Emma wondered what Matt could possibly "need" to talk to her about.

She poured herself the last of the coffee and sat across from him. When Matt pulled out the piece of paper he'd been looking at earlier, her heart slammed to a stop.

He slid the paper across the table so she could get a good look at it. Sure enough, it was a copy of her advertisement. When Emma's heart began to beat again, she held her breath, waiting for Matt to speak.

His voice was low and steely. "Have you lost your mind, Emma?"

Probably.

"Do you have any idea what kind of man might answer this?"

I've been mulling that over.

"What made you do something so crazy?"

Finally, Emma found her voice. "I will not let Douglas Harper take Mandy away from me. He said if I had a husband, there would be no problem. Well, I'm going to find one."

JANET LEE BARTON has lived all over the southern U.S., but she and her husband plan to stay put in southern Mississippi where they have made their home for the past nine years. With three daughters and six grandchildren between them, they feel blessed to have at least one daughter and her family living in the same town. Janet loves being able to share her faith through her writing. Happily married to her very own hero, she is ever thankful that the Lord brought Dan into her life, and she wants to write stories that show that the love between a man and a woman is at its best when the relationship is built with God at the center. She's very happy that the kind of romances the Lord has called her to write can be read by and shared with women of all ages, from teenagers to grandmothers alike.

Books by Janet Lee Barton

HEARTSONG PRESENTS
HP434—Family Circle

A Promise Made

Janet Lee Barton

Heartsong Presents

To my Lord and Savior for showing me the way.

And to my family, whose love and encouragement keep me at it.

I love you and thank God for you all each and every day.

A note from the author:
I love to hear from my readers! You may correspond with me by writing:

> **Janet Lee Barton**
> **Author Relations**
> **PO Box 719**
> **Uhrichsville, OH 44683**

ISBN 1-58660-744-8

A PROMISE MADE

All Scripture quotations are taken from the King James Version of the Bible.

All of the characters and events in this book are fictitious. Any resemblance to actual persons, living or dead, or to actual events is purely coincidental.

PRINTED IN THE U.S.A.

one

Emma finished cleaning the dining room of her café, trying not to worry about Annie, the young mother who worked for her. Annie hadn't seemed to be feeling well on Saturday, and she wasn't in church yesterday. When she didn't shown up for work this morning, Emma couldn't help but be concerned.

At the time she hired Annie, she hadn't really needed an employee, but the seventeen-year-old girl was trying so hard to create a new life for herself, Emma felt compelled to help her. Over a year ago, Annie had knocked on the back door of Emma's café asking for a job. She'd explained that after the death of her parents several years before, when she'd been too young to realize what she was getting into, she'd become a saloon girl. She was living with the consequences of her decision and wanted a better life for the child she was expecting, but she was having a hard time finding decent employment. Emma's heart went out to the young woman, and she'd hired her on the spot.

There were quite a few raised eyebrows from some of her customers when they found a young, unmarried, pregnant woman working at the café, but Emma didn't let that bother her. There were others who reached out to help Annie, too.

Emma's best friend Liddy had moved into Cal's place with her little boy after their marriage a year ago, so Liddy's small

5

but comfortable home had sat empty—until Emma told them about Annie's plight. The couple had generously allowed Annie to move into Liddy's old place, but it was a little way out of town.

Emma was worried about her being out there all alone with the baby, especially if she was sick. If she didn't come in to work tomorrow, Emma would ask the deputy to check on her. He stopped by the café most nights to have a bite to eat before making his rounds.

Emma wished *she* was the reason he came by each night, instead of her cooking. But she'd given up on Deputy Matthew Johnson months ago. She had taken his supper to him at the sheriff's office several times, but he always insisted on paying for it. Said he didn't want to be beholden to anyone. Humph. Emma didn't want him *beholden* to her—she'd rather they be *betrothed!*

She sighed. It just wasn't meant to be. So they shared an easy friendship of sorts. He ate most of his meals at her café, they had common friends around town, and when he came by before starting his rounds at night, they sometimes shared a cup of coffee and conversation. But she realized there was no future for her and Deputy Johnson other than friendship, and her mind had come to terms with it—over and over again.

As the bell above the door jingled and Matthew Johnson entered the café, Emma realized her *heart* hadn't come to the same conclusion. It still beat erratically each time she saw the tall, green-eyed, rusty-haired deputy.

Trying to hide her reaction to his presence, Emma poured him a cup of coffee and dished up the piece of apple pie she'd saved for him. "You weren't out by Annie's place today by any chance, were you?"

Deputy Johnson hung his high-crowned Stetson on the post by the door and crossed the room with long strides. "No. She didn't come in to work?"

Emma shook her head. "I'm worried about her. I think she might be coming down with the influenza that's going around town. If she doesn't come in tomorrow, will you ride out and check on her and Mandy?"

"Certainly." Matt took a seat at his usual table.

"I hate to ask you to go out of your way, but I don't like the idea of her and the baby being out there by themselves, especially if Annie's sick." Emma brought his dessert to the table and sat across from him. "I hope the baby isn't ill."

"I'll ride out tonight just to make sure." Matt took a sip of the hot coffee.

"Thank you, Deputy. It's not like her to miss work."

"She's lucky you gave her a job and that Cal and Liddy provided her with a place to live. Not many around town were willing to do that." Matt forked a piece of pie into his mouth.

"She's an orphan, and I know firsthand how hard that is. I've been on my own a long time, and it can really be a struggle. With a baby on the way, my heart just went out to her. Annie never complains about her lot, though. She tries to make the best life she can for the baby." Emma brought her cup to her mouth and blew away the steam.

"I never thought about it before," Matt said, "but who watches the baby while Annie's working?"

"Oh, Mandy comes with her. We've set up an area in the kitchen for her to play in, and she takes naps upstairs in my apartment. She's an adorable baby. She'll be talking and walking soon. It's no problem to have her here."

"You're a generous woman, Emma."

"I've only done what any good Christian would do," Emma said. "After Annie got baptized in the Hondo River last spring, she really changed. She acknowledged that she'd made some mistakes in her life, and she asked the Lord for His forgiveness. Cal and Liddy and I have only been trying to help Annie make a decent life for herself and Mandy."

Matt snorted. "You three are the only folks I've seen offering to help."

Emma winced inwardly at the bitterness in Matt's voice. "That's not true. The minister and his wife check on her quite often. And the ladies' group made baby clothes for Mandy."

"But you're the only one who offered her a job."

"I don't think she went many places. I mean, how many jobs are there for women in this town?"

"I guess you're right. But I've seen a lot of people around here go to great lengths to cross the street so they wouldn't have to come into contact with Annie."

Emma had noticed the same thing. But those folks would have to answer to the Lord for their actions. Personally, Emma would rather not have some of them in her café at all. She was sure their uppity airs hurt Annie. Not that she ever said anything, but Emma had seen the pain in the girl's eyes.

Matt took a last swallow of coffee and rose to his feet. "Guess I'd better be making my rounds. I'll run out and check on Annie after I finish."

Emma followed him to the door. "Thank you, Deputy."

"You lock up behind me, you hear?"

He put on his Stetson and tipped the wide brim before taking his leave.

Emma locked the door and pulled down the shade. She ambled to the kitchen, rubbing the small of her back and rotating her neck to get the kinks out. It had been a long, busy day. While she may not have needed the help when she hired Annie, business had grown in the last few months, and she sure noticed a difference in the workload when Annie wasn't there. But Matt's assurance that he would check on the young mother and baby relieved her anxiety a bit.

After pumping fresh water into the dishpan, Emma added some of the steaming water that had been simmering on the stove to the dirty dishes, wondering if she'd be by herself the next day. She'd sent home her kitchen helper, Ben, over an hour ago. He hadn't felt well all day, and she hoped he wasn't coming down with the influenza she was afraid Annie had. Emma said a quick prayer that Mandy wouldn't come down with it, too. Maybe she already had, and Annie had stayed home to take care of her. She prayed for them both.

Emma left the dishes to soak while she started her preparations for the next day. She fed her sourdough starter so she would have enough for the next morning's baking, then made sure she had plenty of eggs. She did all the same things she'd been doing for the past several years—but tonight, it suddenly hit her that she was tired of doing it. Tired clear through.

Would she ever have any other kind of life? Here she was twenty-four years old, and it didn't appear she'd be getting married anytime soon. She no longer held out hope that she'd ever become Mrs. Matt Johnson, and she wasn't interested in anyone else.

She might as well give up on having a family. She'd just be Aunt Emma to all of her friends' kids. She adored Annie's baby and Liddy's little son and Cal's two daughters. Still, she longed for children of her own. It had been her dream ever since she'd been orphaned so long ago.

Emma had just started washing the dishes when she heard a loud knock on the back door. Hearing her name called out, she recognized Matt's voice immediately. Though she was sure this wasn't a social call, her pulse began to race and her heart beat double time. She rushed to open the door. "Is Annie all right?"

Matt stood there, tall and handsome, his hat in his hand. "Doc needs you, Emma. Annie's real sick with the influenza. She's asking for you."

Emma grabbed her shawl off the hook near the stairwell and hustled out the door into the chilly mid-September air. "You brought them back with you?"

"No." Matt's expression was grim. "I met her and Mandy on their way in. Sick as she is, she somehow managed to hitch the wagon and start toward Doc's."

"Oh, my." Emma imagined Annie struggling to get into town with Mandy. Hot tears stung her eyes. "How's the baby?"

"She seemed fine."

They scurried down the boardwalk to Doc Bradshaw's office, Emma praying silently all the way that Annie would be all right.

Doc must have been watching for them because he opened the door before they got to it. His thick white hair stood on end, as if he'd been running his fingers through it every which way. Worry clouded his eyes. "I'm glad you're here, Emma. She's been asking for you."

"Where's Mandy?" Emma asked as he led them into his office.

"She's in the kitchen with Myrtle. So far she's not sick, and I'm hoping we can keep her that way. Here, put this on." He helped Emma place a mask over her nose and mouth, then gave another one to Matt. "We don't need you two coming down with this, too."

Doc led them up the hall and into a room where Annie lay flushed with fever, quietly moaning. Matt stayed just inside the door, but Emma rushed to Annie's side and gently brushed aside the thick auburn hair clinging to her damp brow. Annie opened her big brown eyes, and Emma was startled by how bright they were.

"Miss Emma. . .please. . ." Annie's voice was a gravelly whisper.

Emma leaned in close. "I'm here, Annie."

Annie tried to talk again. "Please, take Mandy. . . ."

"Of course. I'll be glad to watch the baby while you're sick."

Annie grasped Emma's wrist and clenched it tightly. "Forever. Promise. . ."

"Shh." Emma covered the young woman's white-knuckled hand with her free one. "You're going to be fine. Just rest so you can get well. I'll take Mandy home with me and care for her until you're feeling better. Don't worry about anything."

"Not going to make it." A sudden spasm of coughing racked Annie's slight body.

Doc rushed to her side and listened to her breathing. He looked up at Emma and shook his head.

When the coughing spell receded, Annie squeezed Emma's hand and continued her plea. "You'll raise Mandy? You are the only one I trust to love her and to raise her to love the Lord. Promise me. Please, Emma."

Emma's heart twisted at the thought that Annie might not make it. She quickly gave the only answer she could. "Yes, yes, I promise. Don't worry about a thing."

"Thank you," Annie whispered before closing her eyes.

Doc listened to Annie's breathing once more, then motioned Emma back into the hall, where Matt had gone to wait for them. Doc closed the door softly. "If she makes it through the night, she may have a chance," Doc said in a low voice. "I'm just not sure she can do that. She's awful weak."

The sob Emma had been holding back finally escaped. "I should have ridden out and checked on her today, or sent Ben, or asked Matt or the sheriff to go out and see if she was all right. If we could have got her here sooner—"

"I don't think it would have made any difference." Doc patted her shoulder. "Annie's been dealing with this for more than a few days. She just couldn't fight it off."

He handed Emma a handkerchief, and she dabbed at her eyes. She tried to pull herself together as they made their way down the hall. In the kitchen, Doc's wife, Myrtle, was sitting at the table, holding Annie's ten-month-old baby in her arms and trying to coax some food into her.

When the baby spotted Emma, she broke into a smile and held out her hands. Emma gathered the child close. "I'm here, Sweetie."

The baby nestled her face into Emma's shoulder.

"Would you like a cup of tea?" Myrtle asked. She gathered her robe around her plump body as she padded to the stove in her slippers.

Emma took a seat at the table and fought tears as Mandy patted her arm. "Yes, please."

Myrtle brought her a cup of tea, then poured coffee for Doc and Matt.

Emma gathered the baby closer. "I should have checked on Annie sooner."

"And I should have gone right out there instead of having

dessert first," Matt added.

"Stop blaming yourselves, you two," Doc said. "It probably wouldn't have changed a thing. You aren't doctors. I can't even do anything about this, except make her as comfortable as possible. We don't have medicine to cure this kind of thing. It comes on fast and hits some people harder than others."

Emma rocked back and forth. When she gazed down at the sweet face framed by strawberry blond curls, she found the baby sound asleep. Emma kissed her head. "Myrtle, do you have a blanket I can wrap her in to get her back to my place? The air is mighty cool tonight."

"She can stay here with us," Myrtle suggested. "I'll be glad to take care of her for a few days."

"Oh, no, thank you," Emma said. "I promised Annie. I'll take her home with me."

Myrtle nodded. "I'll go get a blanket. What about clothes? I might have some of our grandchildren's things."

Emma shook her head. "I already have a few outfits of hers. Since Annie often brought her in to work, we kept several things there. I may have to go out in a few days and get some more. . .if Annie doesn't get better soon."

As Myrtle left the room, Doc got up. "I'll check on her one more time before you leave."

When they were alone, Emma looked up to find Matt watching her.

"Are you all right?" he asked.

"I'm fine. I just. . ." She cleared her throat. "I have to be strong for Mandy's sake."

Matt fingered one of the little girl's curls. "She's sure a pretty baby, isn't she?"

"She certainly is," Myrtle answered for Emma. She came

bustling into the room with a blanket, which she handed to Emma. "And a good baby, too. She sure took to you better than me, though."

Emma draped the blanket around the baby. "She's just more used to me, that's all."

"She's still feverish and sleeping fitfully," Doc said, returning from Annie's sickbed. "I wish I could tell you some good news."

"I'm sure you'll do all you can, Doc." Emma rose to her feet. "I'd better go get Mandy settled in."

Matt stood and opened the front door for her.

"It's awful dark out there," Emma observed. The boardwalk was terribly uneven, and as they'd hustled over to Doc's, she'd almost tripped trying to keep up with Matt. She didn't want to take a chance of falling with the baby in her arms. "Would you mind carrying Mandy for me until we get to the café?"

Matt hesitated for a moment, then awkwardly took the baby into his arms. Emma was sure he felt uncomfortable, like most single men would. But she felt just as inexperienced. *At least he's familiar with the streets at night,* she thought. Mandy would be safer with the deputy than with her.

Emma turned to Doc and Myrtle. "Thank you for taking care of Mandy until I could get here."

"No thanks needed, Dear," Myrtle said, walking them to the door.

Matt led the way down the street to her café, and once inside, he followed Emma up the stairs and into her apartment. He quickly transferred the baby into Emma's arms. "I'll wait downstairs until you get her settled. . .unless you need me to do anything up here?"

Emma could tell he felt uneasy in her living quarters. "No, we're fine. You don't need to stay."

Matt backed out the door. "I'll wait for you to lock up."

Emma pulled her bedcovers down with one hand and laid the baby in the middle, surrounding her with every pillow she could find. She was thankful that Mandy stayed asleep. *The poor baby must be exhausted having others take care of her,* Emma thought as she brushed a kiss over the child's forehead.

Aware that Matt was waiting for her, she made her way downstairs and was surprised to find him at her kitchen sink washing the dishes. "You don't have to do that."

He grinned as he scrubbed a pan. "I figured I could do something useful while I was waiting."

Emma grabbed a clean towel and began to dry the dishes he'd washed. "It helps a lot. Thank you."

Matt rinsed the pot and placed it on the drain board. "You're welcome. The baby's all settled down?"

"She never woke up. Maybe she'll sleep through the night."

"I hope so. . .for both your sakes." After handing the last pot to Emma to dry, Matt emptied the dishpan and wiped it out.

Emma set the pot on a shelf beside the stove and spread the towel over the edge of the sink while Matt retrieved his hat from the hook. "You've been real good to Annie," he said, fingering the brim. "She obviously thinks a lot of you."

Emma followed him to the door. "Please pray for her. . .and for Mandy."

"I will," he promised. "You try to get some rest, you hear? And lock up as soon as I leave."

"Thank you for coming to get me and for helping me bring Mandy home." Emma was sure he'd only assisted out of a sense of professional duty, but that didn't matter. She was grateful she hadn't had to deal with all this alone.

"I'm glad I could help. Good night."

"Good night." Emma closed the door behind him and locked it. She glanced around the kitchen to make sure there was nothing else she needed to do for the next day, wondering what tomorrow would bring.

Expelling a deep breath, she climbed back up the stairs to the bedroom. Emma gazed down on the innocent little face, so peaceful in slumber. It hurt to think about the possibility that Annie might not make it—that this sweet baby could become an orphan. Emma understood all too well what that was like. Because she did, she fully intended to keep the promise she'd made to Annie, if it came to that. She might not have the first idea how to be a mother, but she'd do her best for this precious baby.

Dear God, please help Annie. And help me be strong for Mandy. In Jesus' name, amen.

❧

Matt waited to hear Emma lock the door before he started his rounds. When she'd looked up at him with that worried expression, he'd been sorely tempted to pull her into his arms, kiss her furrowed brow, and tell her everything would be fine. But he didn't have the right.

Did she have any idea how his pulse raced whenever she blushed at him? He'd been attracted to her for longer than he wanted to think about. Tonight, he couldn't seem to get her out of his mind.

Matt jiggled the doorknob of the barbershop down the street from the café, checking to make sure Homer Williams had locked up. He did the same thing to half a dozen other businesses, not really thinking about what he was doing, just working out of habit.

Emma was one of the prettiest women he'd ever met, with her dark hair and blue eyes. She was also one of the kindest women he knew. She'd help anyone in trouble, and that was a fact. If his mind could be changed about taking a wife, it would be by Emma Hanson. Of course, he wasn't going to change his mind, but she sure would be a catch for some lucky man. The thought left a bad taste in Matt's mouth.

Matt vividly recalled the day his father had died from being shot in the line of duty. His mother had grieved deeply over his death. But she'd worked her fingers to the bone, taking in wash for everyone in town, in order to raise Matt and his brothers until they were all grown and on their own. She was the reason he'd promised himself he'd never marry. Having taken up his father's line of work, he was well aware of the dangers inherent to his profession. He would not leave a widow behind to work herself to death.

Matt strolled into the Oasis, one of the two saloons at the end of Main Street and the only one with lights still on inside. "How's it goin', Sam?" he asked the burly manager.

"Oh, pretty good," Sam said, wiping down the highly polished bar. "Nobody cheated at cards tonight, and I didn't have to throw anyone out."

"That's good to hear."

Other than Sam, the bar was unoccupied. Matt felt grateful for the quiet night. He already had too much on his mind.

"I'm about ready to close up here," Sam said. "Can I get you anything?"

"No, thanks," Matt said. "You go on home to that pretty wife of yours."

Sam grabbed a jacket off the wall peg. "Think I'll do just that."

After saying good night, Matt resumed his rounds along the opposite side of the street. The town was peaceful, with crickets providing the only sound.

He passed the fire department, which was across the street from Emma's café. Then, at the next building, he opened the door to the sheriff's office. Matt poured himself a cup of thick coffee and took it outside to lean against the hitching post. The large front window with *Emma's Café* etched in gold was dark, but light still shone from the window of her living quarters upstairs. He wondered if the baby was awake.

That sweet woman would be taking on a huge responsibility if Annie didn't make it. Emma had never had a child of her own, never even been married. It certainly wasn't the best situation. Yet tonight, when she took Mandy from him, the expression on her face was so tender, so protective.

He'd never thought of Emma as maternal or domestic. She was one of the best cooks around, but he considered her more of a businesswoman than a homemaker. He'd been surprised at the cozy feel to her apartment—so much so that he'd hightailed it out of there as fast as he could. No, after tonight, he could never think of Emma Hanson in quite the same way again.

two

The first night was a long one. Although the baby stayed asleep, Emma woke often, afraid she'd roll over on Mandy or wouldn't hear her if she woke up. Mostly she tossed and turned, wondering if she'd lost her senses.

How could she have promised Annie she would raise Mandy? What did she know about taking care of a baby? Emma prayed even harder that Annie would get well.

Emma tried to remember everything she'd seen Annie do for Mandy during the day, and all she'd seen Liddy do with her and Cal's children.

She was glad Annie had weaned Mandy early so she wouldn't have to worry about that. The ten-month-old baby could drink out of a cup and was already trying to feed herself with a spoon. But it wasn't feeding or changing or clothing Mandy that had Emma so frightened. It was the responsibility of teaching Mandy to love the Lord and to live life the way He and Annie would want her to that overwhelmed her.

When Mandy woke before dawn, needing to be changed and missing her mama, Emma didn't have time to worry about the kind of job she was doing. She simply saw to the baby's needs, then cuddled her close until her crying subsided. She was glad the baby was used to being around her.

Emma dressed quickly and pinned her hair up in a knot on top of her head, then picked up the baby and descended the stairs with Mandy on her hip. She'd have to get one of those new telephones installed as soon as possible, she decided, so she could call Doc regularly to check on Annie, and to get in touch with him if Mandy got sick.

She hoped Ben would be well enough to come to work. She should probably try to find someone else to help out so she could pay more attention to the baby.

As she slipped Mandy into her high chair and donned an apron, Emma thanked the Lord that Annie had been bringing Mandy to work with her. Ben had fenced off an area in one corner of the kitchen for the baby to play in, and several of Mandy's favorite toys lay scattered throughout the space.

Emma took a deep breath as she prepared Mandy's breakfast and fed her before starting preparations for the café. She set the baby in her play area, and for the moment she seemed all right, occupied with her toys. But Emma was sure she'd start missing her mama soon.

Emma mixed up a batch of biscuits and cut them out, telling herself over and over that she could do this. With the Lord's help, of course.

A knock on the back door startled her, but when she opened the door and found Matt standing there, she braced herself for bad news.

"Annie made it through the night, but Doc still doesn't hold out much hope."

Emma's heart sank, and she fought the urge to cry.

Matt peeked into the kitchen. "How's Mandy doing?"

Emma stepped to the side and motioned Matt to come in. "She slept through the night but woke up crying. Bless her heart, she doesn't understand what's going on." Emma poured two cups of coffee. As she handed one to Matt, she noticed him watching her closely.

"You didn't get much sleep last night, did you?" he asked.

"Not much," she admitted.

"How are you going to run the café and take care of Mandy?"

Emma shrugged. "Ben will help. And I can hire another person. I promised Annie I'd do this, and I will."

"But—"

There was another knock on the back door, and Emma was glad to have the conversation interrupted. What little confidence she'd been feeling was quickly deteriorating.

Emma was relieved to open the door to Ben.

"Mornin', Miss Emma. How are you today?"

"Better now that you're here. We've got a problem."

"Oh?" Ben tied on his apron. If he was surprised to see Matt or Mandy in the kitchen, he didn't show it.

"Annie is real sick. Deputy Johnson says Doc doesn't think she'll get better. And I promised to take care of Mandy."

Ben nodded. "Don't you worry, Miss Emma. You can do it."

At least Ben thought she could handle things. "Thank you, Ben. Are you feeling all right? I was worried you might have come down with the influenza, too."

"I'm fine. Sure am sorry about Miss Annie, though. I hope Doc is wrong. She's a nice lady." Ben began to slice the bacon for the customers who'd be coming in soon.

Matt drained his cup and put on his hat. "I'd better be getting back to work. I'll check on Annie later and give you an update. Is there anything you need me to do?"

Emma couldn't keep the cool tone out of her voice as she answered, "No, thank you."

He watched Mandy play for a moment. "If you do need anything, just have Ben find me."

Emma released a deep breath as he walked out the door. She didn't have time to worry about what Deputy Matthew Johnson thought about her keeping Mandy. She had a full day ahead of her.

As if Ben could read her thoughts, he said, "Don't you worry, Miss Emma. I can work the front and the kitchen while you take care of the baby. We can do it."

Emma smiled at the man who'd helped her for the past five years. "Thank you, Ben. I'm sure you're right."

&

Matt almost shivered as he walked away from Emma's. She'd become distant as soon as he asked her how she was going to handle everything. He hadn't meant to make her feel bad, but he honestly had no idea how she was going to run her business and take care of Annie's child at the same time.

Matt made his morning rounds, glad he'd be off duty soon. It had been a long night.

He watched portly Douglas Harper open up his bank down the street. The morning train's whistle could be heard in the distance.

"Mornin', Deputy," Homer Williams greeted as he unlocked his barbershop. "Looks like it's going to be a nice day."

"Indeed it does," Matt said, glancing up. The sky was a clear blue, with only a wisp of a cloud floating in it. The sun shone brightly, promising a warm day.

Matt ambled over to the sheriff's office. He hoped Annie would be feeling better today. But deep inside, he doubted that would be the case. Doc had said she'd been sick for longer than any of them realized.

&

The morning passed in a blur as Emma balanced her time

between taking care of the breakfast crowd and checking on Mandy. The baby had played herself to sleep in the middle of the rush, just as she always did. Emma hoped she'd be able to check on Annie when things slowed down.

By the time the morning crowd thinned out, Emma was beginning to feel the effects of her sleepless night. When her best friend Liddy McAllister came in with the cakes and pies she baked for the café, Emma made a valiant effort to greet her in her normal, cheery way.

"Emma!" Liddy cried, leading her to a table and insisting that she sit. "Myrtle told me about Annie. Did you get any sleep at all last night? You certainly don't look like you did."

Emma couldn't help but chuckle. Usually it was Liddy who possessed a bushel full of tact, while Emma sometimes spoke before she thought. . .but not today. "Thank you, Liddy. Now I realize why my customers were staring at me strangely."

Liddy poured them each a cup of coffee and sat across from Emma. "I'm just concerned. Have you had any news about Annie?"

Emma took a sip of the hot coffee. "Not since this morning. I should go over and check on her."

"I'll do that. You should take a nap."

Emma stifled a yawn. "Mandy will be awake and hungry soon."

"Em. . .I saw Matt. He said you're planning on keeping Mandy if Annie doesn't make it."

Emma lifted her chin. Obviously Matt didn't think she could do it. Was that how her friend felt, too? She peered into Liddy's eyes. "I am."

Liddy rested her jaw in her hand. "I see that."

"And?"

"And nothing. You'll do a wonderful job. It won't be easy, but you know that from watching me. And I'll help in any way I can."

"Thank you, Liddy. I am a bit scared."

Liddy patted Emma's hand. "You'll do fine. Don't you remember how frightened I was about raising a baby? You were there."

"And no help at all."

"You were more help than you realize," Liddy said. "When I was alone with my son, I fell apart. But Cal helped me with my fears and assured me that God would give me the right instincts, and I just needed to follow them."

"But you are your son's natural mother, Liddy. I'm—"

"You are a woman who will be a wonderful mother. . . whether the child is given to you or if it's your own. I would trust you with my children in a minute."

Emma blinked back tears. "Oh, Liddy. Thank you. I really needed to hear that."

❧

The next few days were some of the hardest Emma had ever gone through. She got a telephone installed on the wall next to the stairs, so she was able to check on Annie several times during the day. But the news was never good. Annie didn't get better. She slipped into a coma, and Doc said it was only a matter of time.

The first night taking care of Mandy was easy compared to the next two. She was a good baby, but she missed her mama, and she woke up crying several times each night. Emma cried with her as she rocked, cuddled, and bonded with the child. She'd loved her as Annie's child. Now she was beginning to love her as her own as she took care of her needs and gave her the attention Annie would if she could.

Emma realized it was only with God's help that she made it through each day. She and Ben managed to run the café without too many snags, but she didn't imagine it would get any easier.

"Miss Emma," Ben said as he swept the floor at the end of the day, "I know someone who needs a job, and we could sure use the help. You've got your hands full with that baby, and you have to get some rest."

"You're right. I've been thinking about putting up a help-wanted sign, but I kept thinking Annie was going to get better."

"It ain't gonna happen, Miss Emma."

She sighed, her heart heavy. "Who do you have in mind?"

"Well, you remember my brother died last year? His widow, Hallie, has been takin' in wash, doin' cleanin' at the hotels, and whatever she can to make a livin', but they only use her when one of their regular helpers is sick. She'd be glad to help out here, and she could sure use some steady work."

"Your recommendation is good enough for me. Tell Hallie to come see me tomorrow."

Ben grinned. "You won't be sorry, Miss Emma. Hallie's a hard worker."

But Hallie didn't come in the next day. Annie died during the night, and Emma closed the café in her honor.

❧

The following day Emma stood at the grave site, holding Mandy tightly, weeping silently while the minister officiated. She thanked the Lord that Mandy was too young to understand the heart-wrenching changes going on in her little life.

Deputy Johnson stood behind her, giving Emma comfort, although she was sure he was unaware of it. She was pleased at the good turnout of church members and a few customers Annie had waited on regularly. But Emma had never felt more relief than when she'd been able to leave the graveyard behind.

The band of mourners made their way back to town, and most everyone came to the café for the noon meal. Several church members had brought in food before the funeral. Emma's heart was touched when Ben shooed her out of her own kitchen, and, along with some of the women from church, made sure everyone was served.

Cal and Liddy's children entertained Mandy. While the baby enjoyed their attention, her gaze constantly sought out Emma, as if to make sure she was still there. Emma made certain to say something reassuring to the baby or reach out and touch her head each time she passed by their table.

As people began to leave, Douglas Harper, head of Harper Bank and one of the town's councilmen, approached Emma with hat in hand. "Miss Emma, it's a wonderful thing you did, taking in that little girl. We'll make permanent arrangements for her in the next few weeks."

"What do you mean?" Emma frowned, immediately suspicious of this man.

Several years back Mr. Harper had tried to buy her place of business. Her café was in a prime location, near the train depot, across from the sheriff's office, and just a couple of blocks from the Roswell Hotel. But she had no intention of selling her property. Harper had been persistent, and Emma'd had to work hard to convince him that her *no* meant *no*.

Just a couple of years ago, Harper had caused no end of trouble for Liddy, too, trying to foreclose on her farm after her first husband died. Why, that horrible man had even gone so far as to try to blackmail Liddy into marrying him!

Emma considered Douglas Harper a real snake in the grass. She wondered what he was up to now.

"We'll have to try to find a family to take her in, or get her into the orphanage in Santa Fe," he said.

"There's no need for that, Mr. Harper. I promised Annie I would raise Mandy, and I intend to do just that."

"No one is going to hold you to a deathbed promise."

"I hold myself to it."

Matt crossed the room to stand at her side. His nearness provided a sense of relief.

"Miss Emma," Harper said coolly, "you're a single woman. It doesn't seem fitting for you—"

"Mr. Harper," Matt interrupted him, "perhaps this isn't the time to discuss this. Miss Emma has had a long few days."

"There won't be a good time to discuss this," Emma said.

Liddy McAllister appeared at Emma's side. "Emma, I haven't seen you eat a bite. Come on. You need to—"

"I'm not hungry."

Liddy took hold of her arm and gently pulled her away from the banker. "I understand. But Mandy needs you now. You have to keep up your strength."

That was all it took. "You're right." Emma turned back to Matt and Councilman Harper. "Excuse me, gentlemen. There are some things I need to take care of." With that, she allowed Liddy to lead her to a table where a plate of food sat waiting for her.

❧

"Well!" Harper said. "If she thinks the town leaders are going to let a single woman keep that child, she's sadly mistaken. This isn't the end of things by a long shot." The banker stomped off.

Much as he hated to agree with Douglas Harper on anything, this time Matt felt the man was right. It would be a huge responsibility for Emma to take on, as busy as she was with the café.

But it was going to be really hard for Emma to give up Annie's baby. And today was not the right time to press the issue. Matt took a plate of food and made his way over to Emma's table, where Cal and Liddy were keeping her company.

"No one is going to take Mandy away from me," Emma was saying. "No one."

Liddy patted her shoulder. "Of course not. Don't you give it another thought, Em." But her eyes held a worried look as she glanced at Matt and Cal.

Matt had never felt so confused in his life. He wanted to support the woman he cared so much about. But how could he do that? This baby wasn't even Emma's. She didn't know what she was letting herself in for, trying to raise someone else's child and running a business on her own.

Perhaps if the idea came from him instead of Harper, Emma would at least consider it. "If they could find a couple to take her in," he asked hesitantly, "wouldn't that be better for Mandy?"

The silence that fell on the table was deafening. Emma stopped pushing food around on her plate, put down her fork, and glared up at Matt. "Annie asked *me* to raise Mandy. She didn't ask me to find a couple to take her. She didn't ask anyone else. You were there, Deputy Johnson. You heard her. I can and I *will* give Mandy love and security. I will keep my promise."

Emma stood and gathered the baby in her arms. "If you don't mind, it's been a long day. I think I'll put Mandy down for a nap."

Matt felt as if he'd been slapped as he watched Emma leave. Cal and Liddy shook their heads at him.

"Are you two going to tell me you don't think a married couple wouldn't be better for Mandy?"

"I will tell you that your timing is really bad," Cal said. "And that Emma will make a wonderful mother for that baby. Annie believed that, or she never would have asked her to take Mandy."

Matt had never felt so confused in his life. Even Cal and Liddy didn't seem to realize he was only thinking of Emma.

"Raising a child alone is hard," Liddy said, "but it can be done. Happens all the time. And Emma won't be single forever," she added, raising her eyebrows at Matt.

Liddy sent her two girls to work in the kitchen, gathered up her toddler son, and hurried upstairs to check on her friend.

❧

Emma was rocking Mandy to sleep when Liddy entered the sitting room. She brushed at her wet lashes.

Liddy hugged her friend. "Aw, Em. It's going to be all right."

Emma sniffed. "I hope I stop all this weeping soon. I don't know when I've cried so much."

"Losing a friend is heartbreaking. And when a child is left behind, it's even more so." Liddy rubbed her friend's shoulders.

"I'm afraid I'm going to lose Mandy. Harper wants to take her away from me. And judging from Matt's reaction, Harper's not alone in his opinions." Emma held Mandy closer and kissed the top of her head. "I've grown to love this little girl. I can't let her go. I won't—no matter how hard I have to fight to keep her."

three

Much to Emma's relief, Hallie came to work the next day. Her ready smile and sparkling eyes told Emma she'd be crazy not to hire her. Hallie would work on a part-time basis, coming in most days to help with the noontime rush. From the first day, she assisted Ben in the kitchen and also helped watch the baby, leaving Emma free to take care of the front. Ben was right. She was a hard worker, and she was wonderful with Mandy.

Emma tried to get used to the changes in her life. Caring for Mandy and running a business was a challenge, but Emma had always met the challenges in her life head-on. This time would be no exception.

She had a feeling it was only a matter of time until Councilman Harper would make trouble. The next town meeting was scheduled for the following week.

She'd noticed several of her patrons whispering when they didn't think she was paying attention, and she'd overheard her name and Annie's several times. Some of the people expressed concern about her raising the child "all alone." Everyone had advice to give. Emma was learning to ignore most of it.

She and Mandy were adjusting to each other more quickly than Emma had expected. The baby was sleeping better and began calling her "Em-mama." Emma promised herself she would keep Annie's memory alive for Mandy as best she could, but it would be several years before Mandy could begin to understand what had happened to her mother.

Liddy and Cal brought in Annie's few personal belongings from her house. It wasn't much, but someday the items would mean a great deal to Mandy. There was a picture of Annie, a Bible the church had given her on the day she'd been baptized, several hand-crocheted items, including a beautiful tablecloth, and Annie's clothes. Emma packed everything away carefully.

There was very little clothing for the baby, and Mandy was quickly growing out of what she did have. Emma wasn't much of a seamstress, but a new dry goods store had recently opened in town, so she and Mandy went shopping together during an afternoon lull at the café.

Emma also went to Jaffa-Prager Company, Roswell's large general store, to order a baby carriage and a crib. She was quite pleased with her purchases and was eager to show off the new clothes she'd bought for Mandy.

But the only patron in the café when she returned made her heart beat triple-time, betraying her emotions. She wasn't inclined to brag to Matt about her purchases. Still, she couldn't bring herself to be rude to him, either.

"Afternoon, Deputy," Emma said.

"How are you two today?" Matt asked.

Emma juggled Mandy on her hip as she filled a cup with milk for the child. "We're fine, aren't we, Mandy? We've been shopping for new clothes, haven't we?"

Mandy bobbed her head, and Emma wondered how much she understood.

"And you are going to look just beautiful in everything, aren't you, Darling?" Emma tickled the baby under her chin.

When Mandy giggled, Emma and Matt both chuckled, and the tension between them seemed to ease.

"How is she adjusting?" Matt asked, reaching out to touch Mandy's cheek.

"She's doing well. Sleeping better. Not crying so much." She watched Mandy grin at Matt's overtures.

"That's good." He peered at Emma. "How are you doing?"

She shrugged. "I'm doing well. Sleeping better. Not crying so much."

Matt chuckled, and so did Mandy. "I'm glad."

Emma laughed outright when Mandy echoed, "Gad."

Matt raised an eyebrow. "She's talking?"

"Only a few words here and there." She bent to kiss the top of Mandy's head. "She calls me Em-mama."

Mandy pointed at her. "Em-mama."

"That's sweet," Matt said.

"I think so."

Hallie came in from the kitchen. "Do you want I should take her, Miss Emma?"

"No, thank you, Hallie. I need to go up and change clothes. Just refill the deputy's coffee cup."

Matt shook his head. "No more for me, thanks. I have to get back to work."

"I'll be in the kitchen if you need me, Miss Emma," Hallie said as she returned to her work.

Emma stood with the baby while Matt drained his cup and put his hat back on. He ruffled Mandy's hair. "I'm glad she's adjusting well. It's obvious you're taking good care of her. But you seem awful tired. Try to get some rest, won't you?"

"I'm fine, thank you," Emma returned coolly.

Matt left money for his pie and coffee on the table, then walked to the door. "Bye-bye, Mandy," he said at the doorway. "See you later."

After the deputy left, Emma slowly climbed upstairs, holding Mandy. She *was* tired. But she wasn't about to admit it to
Matt. After all, he might be in cahoots with Harper. Her heart
twisted at the thought.

She held the baby closer. She might never have the complete family she'd dreamed of, but because Annie trusted her
child to her, she would be a mother to this precious child, and
they would be a family. Emma kissed the top of Mandy's
head, praying that she would be able to keep this child she'd
grown to love.

&

On Sunday, Emma said a silent prayer for guidance as she
entered church with Mandy on her hip. It was one thing to
disregard the hushed comments of her patrons, but quite
another to ignore those same stares and whispers from some
of her church family.

She held her head high and gathered Mandy closer, overwhelmed by the protective feeling that rose in her chest. She
quickly made her way down the aisle to sit in the pew behind
Liddy and Cal. Their daughters, Amy and Grace, waved and
grinned at Mandy, and they received a small giggle in return.

Liddy leaned over the back of the pew. "You will you be
having dinner with us, won't you, Em? The children can't
wait to play with Mandy again."

Emma smiled at her friend, thankful that businesses in this
town all closed on Sundays. "Thank you, Liddy. We'd love to
come out to your place for dinner."

She did have some loyal friends in this town, and she had
no doubt they would stand beside her in her fight to keep
Mandy. As the service got under way, she reminded herself
that the most important thing was that God was on her side in

this. He had brought Annie into her life, and He'd heard Emma's promise. She was sure He would help her keep it.

When she left the church, the minister, John Turley, stopped her. "Emma," he said, his arm wrapped around his wife, Caroline, "we just wanted to tell you we're proud of the way you stepped in and agreed to take Mandy for Annie."

"And if there's anything we can do to help you," Caroline added, "please call on us. We'll be praying for you both."

"Thank you," Emma said. "That means more than I can say."

Several other members of the church expressed similar sentiments, and their encouragement strengthened her. In fact, that afternoon was one of the most relaxing she could remember since before Annie passed away.

Emma sat on Liddy and Cal's front porch, enjoying a cup of coffee and a slice of Liddy's apple pie while the children played together. It warmed Emma's heart to hear the baby's chuckles as the older girls played patty-cake and sang songs to her. She knew there would be tough times ahead, but spending the day with supportive friends did much to strengthen her resolve.

❧

Emma wasn't a bit surprised when toward the end of the next week; she received a personal invitation to attend the town council meeting scheduled for the upcoming Monday evening.

"To discuss the custody of Mandy Drake," the letter said.

Humph! They could discuss all they wanted to, but she was keeping Annie's baby and that was all there was to it.

Emma tried not to worry about it. She was much too busy to fret, anyway. When the situation did enter her thoughts, she gave it to the Lord and got on with taking care of Mandy and her business.

The night of the meeting, Cal and Liddy showed up at the café to escort her and give her their support. Emma was thankful for their presence. She'd prayed all day, but she was still nervous to the point of feeling sick to her stomach. She trusted the Lord to get her through the evening and to give her the strength to handle whatever happened. Still, she felt as if she were fighting for her very life. . .and for that of her young charge.

Hallie offered to watch Mandy during the meeting, but Emma didn't want to let the child out of her sight. After donning her Sunday best, a two-piece navy brocade, she dressed the baby in one of her new outfits and cuddled her close as she walked down the boardwalk, with Cal and Liddy flanking her protectively.

When they entered the town hall, Emma gathered Mandy close. She raised her chin a notch as she realized all eyes were on her and the baby she held. It seemed half the town had shown up for this meeting. There must have been at least fifty chairs set out in rows, and most of them were already taken. Several men stood next to the windows that lined each side of the room.

Sheriff Haynes, a tall, middle-aged man with dark hair and alert brown eyes, stood at the back of the room. Matt leaned against the wall near the side door with Deputy Carmichael, a young man with blond hair and blue eyes. Matt tipped his hat as her glance caught his. Determined to ignore the thumping of her heart at the sight of him, she turned her head and looked for a seat.

Doc Bradshaw waved at Emma from the front row. His wife, Myrtle, patted the empty seat beside her. Emma joined them, adjusting Mandy on her lap, and Liddy and Cal took the seats next to her. She was confident these four people would stand up for her, but as the meeting was called to order, Emma wasn't sure their support would really help.

Four council members sat at a rectangular table at the front of the room. Harper stood beside the table, talking to the men in hushed tones. Homer Williams, the owner of the barbershop down the street from Emma's café, would probably vote whatever way Harper did.

Carl Adams sat beside Homer. He owned a big ranch outside of town but lived in Roswell because his wife hated the country. He came into the café fairly often, and Emma thought he might vote for her to keep Mandy, but she couldn't be sure.

Emma didn't know the other two councilmen, Ed Bagley and John McDonald, well enough to speculate what they might think.

Emma wondered why the other three town councilmen weren't in attendance. Then she remembered that the mayor had gone back East to settle his parents' estate, and the other two members were out of town on vacation.

Harper peered at his watch and took the podium. He immediately launched into a plea of help for Emma, telling the citizens that as a single woman running a business, she shouldn't be "saddled" with a baby. "What we really need is a couple who is willing to take the child—just until we can make arrangements to get her to the orphanage in Santa Fe. Surely one or two of you couples can come forward to do that?"

Emma gathered Mandy in her arms and stood to her feet to address the crowded room. "It appears Councilman Harper isn't quite clear on Mandy's situation. I promised Annie I would raise her, and I intend to do just that. I can run a business and raise a child. I do not want anyone to take Mandy." The baby fidgeted and Emma sat back down, rocking her.

"But Miss Emma," Mr. Harper said, "you are a single woman. This child needs two parents."

Doc Bradshaw stood. "Harper, this baby was doing just fine with the one parent she had. And I heard Emma promise Annie she would take her."

"Yes, well, she didn't leave a will, Doc. A deathbed request does not constitute a legal declaration of intent."

Doc grunted and took his seat.

Minister Turley, who was sitting with his wife two rows back, spoke up. "I'd venture to say that most of us don't have a written will. A deathbed request is often all there's time for."

"That brings another thought to bear," Harper interrupted. "We don't really know much about Annie Drake. Since the child comes from an uncertain background, it's even more important that she be placed into a stable home with two parents."

"Harper, what's gotten into you?" Doc sputtered. "What have you got against this child?"

Harper pointed to Mandy. "She could be the daughter of an outlaw, for all we know. Her character is, at best, questionable."

Emma jumped to her feet, startling Mandy a bit. "Are you saying that *my* character is questionable as well? After all, I was an orphan, too." She stroked the baby's head as she glared at Harper.

"No, of course not," the councilman said. "We all know you. But we have no idea who the father of this child was. . .and there's no telling what kind of person she'll become."

"I can tell you right now, Mandy will grow up to be a fine Christian woman if I am allowed to raise her in the way Annie asked me to."

Homer Williams stood. "Miss Emma, we understand your intentions are honorable. But we are concerned that you might be taking on more than you are able—"

"Mr. Williams, with God all things are possible," Emma asserted.

Homer cleared his throat and focused his attention on the rest of the group. "We need a married couple who is willing to take this child for a few weeks. Surely, that's not too much to ask."

Emma scanned the crowd, making eye contact with as many as would meet her gaze. She saw Jim Harrison nudge his wife, Nelda. Nelda glared at her husband. Harold Ferguson started to raise his hand, but his wife, Beatrice, quickly pulled it back down. Several silent conversations took place between husbands and wives. After what seemed like forever, Emma breathed a sigh of relief. Not one hand stayed up. She promised herself she would thank these women as soon as possible.

Homer sat back down and crossed his arms.

Harper raised an eyebrow. "No one? Surely one of you fine, upstanding women could take the child for a few weeks."

Liddy spoke up. "Emma Hanson is perfectly capable of taking care of Mandy. There is no need to do this."

"The town leaders believe there is, Mrs. McAllister." Harper's sinister gaze shifted from Liddy to Cal.

Cal stood. "The town leaders need to rethink, then," he said, his hand on his wife's shoulder as if protecting her from whatever the rude banker might say next.

Harper turned his focus back to the men at the table. "We have discussed this at length, haven't we, gentlemen?"

Homer and Ed nodded. The other two councilmen kept

their heads down. Emma began to wonder just who ran this town.

"If you were a married woman," Harper continued, "there would be no question of you keeping the baby. But we feel it would be in the child's best interest to have two parents. We are contacting the orphanage in Santa Fe. When we hear back from them, we will make arrangements to take the baby there. In the meantime, since no one has come forward. . .we will allow you to take care of the baby."

Emma bit her tongue and prayed for guidance. But she couldn't keep the sarcasm out of her voice as she said, "Thank you so much, Councilman." She started to leave, but stopped mid-aisle and whirled back around to face the council members. "I want you all to know I have no intention of giving this baby up. With me, a promise made is a promise kept."

"Well, we'll just see about that," Douglas Harper muttered.

❧

Matt stood in the doorway of the sheriff's office and stared at the town council building down the street. The lights in the windows told him the meeting was still in progress.

He agreed with the council members that Emma shouldn't be raising Mandy, but that was only because he knew how hard it would be on her. He'd watched her closely these past few weeks. She'd been a wonderful mother to that baby.

She'd appeared so vulnerable when she walked in with Mandy. He was glad Cal and Liddy had accompanied her. But he was angry at the way Harper had treated her. He'd wanted to come to her defense, but the memories of his own mother struggling to raise him and his brothers kept him quiet.

Matt had left the room in the middle of the meeting. Sheriff Haynes and Deputy Carmichael would let him know if any problems came up. Besides, even though he didn't think Emma should raise the baby alone, he couldn't stand there and watch Harper try to take Mandy away.

He watched from the office until he saw Emma leave the building, with Mandy held close. Cal and Liddy were right behind her. From the smiles on their faces, he guessed things hadn't gone quite the way Harper had planned. And at that moment. . .he was glad.

❧

Emma shook like a leaf as she scurried down the boardwalk. She couldn't wait to get Mandy back to the café.

Cal called to her. "Emma, slow down."

She stopped and turned. "I'm sorry. I—"

"It's all right, Em," Liddy said as they continued walking together.

"I think I'm going to have to run for councilman next time a position opens up," Cal said. "I thought our council was made of stronger stuff."

"So did I," Liddy said. "I'm sure the mayor would never let this happen."

"I don't understand why Harper is so set on taking Mandy away from me." Emma rubbed the child's back. "No one will take better care of her than I will. I'm not going to let it happen. I won't allow anyone to take Mandy away from me—especially not that snake, Douglas Harper!"

four

Matt scrambled to catch up to Emma as she hurried toward the café, Liddy and Cal keeping pace beside her. Just before he reached them, Emma whirled around, almost smacking into him. Anger reddened her cheeks.

"Well, Deputy, I noticed you didn't stay to hear the outcome of the meeting."

"I can see you still have Mandy, so—"

"I hope you're prepared to arrest me," Emma interrupted, "because you might have to before this is all over."

"Em—" He touched her arm, but she jerked away, still holding the baby tight. "I'm sure it won't come to that."

"I'm not," Emma huffed. "Harper means to take Mandy away from me, but I'll go to jail before I'll give her up."

Liddy put her arm around Emma. "You're not going to jail. Now, let's get a cup of coffee and a piece of that pecan pie I brought in earlier, all right?"

Emma took a deep breath. "You're right. I do need to calm down so I can figure out my next move."

The ladies continued on down the boardwalk, and the men followed. Cal filled Matt in on what had happened after he left the meeting.

When Emma stopped at the door of the café, Matt was sure she was going to tell him to go away. Instead, her expression was soft and remorseful.

"I'm sorry, Deputy. My tirade was uncalled for. You're

welcome to join us for coffee and pie if you like."

When she looked at him with those beautiful blue eyes, Matt wanted nothing more than to take her up on her offer. But she still seemed to think he was against her. "Thank you for the invitation, but I'm on duty. If you're all still here when I get through making my rounds, I might stop in."

Cal slapped him on the shoulder. "See you later, then. Hope your night is uneventful."

"So do I." Matt tipped his hat to the women. "Evening, ladies."

"Night, Matt," Liddy said.

"Good night, Deputy." Emma swept up her skirts and entered the café.

❧

Emma couldn't decide if she was relieved or disappointed that Matt hadn't come in. She chided herself for wanting him around even though he disapproved of her keeping Mandy. She shouldn't care one fig what the deputy did or said. Of course, she'd been telling herself that for months, to no avail. She did care—too much.

Hallie came out of the kitchen just as they walked in. Emma let her take Mandy to the kitchen to play awhile before bedtime. Since no customers were in the café, Emma decided to close early. Liddy poured coffee and brought plates of pie to the table.

Cal handed Emma a piece of paper with a name printed on it. "I don't know if you'll be needing a lawyer, but I know an honest one. If you go see him, tell him we sent you."

"Thank you." Emma slipped the piece of paper into her skirt pocket. "Cal, do you think Matt is in cahoots with Douglas Harper?"

Cal shook his head. "I'm sure he doesn't like the man any better than we do."

"But Matt agrees that I shouldn't be raising Mandy."

"I don't think that's the case," Liddy said. "He's just concerned about you trying to raise Mandy on your own. But I told him that if anyone could do it, you could."

"Thank you. I don't imagine you changed his mind."

"I'm not sure. But I can't believe he'd be working with Harper."

"I hope not," Emma said. "You know, the town council should have more important things to do than try to take an orphan away from someone who wants to raise her."

Liddy patted Emma's hand. "Everything will be all right."

"I pray it is. I'll leave town before I'll let them take her."

"It's not going to get to that point. You have a lot of friends here. Give them a chance to act on your behalf."

Emma chuckled, remembering the expression on Alma Burton's face when her husband tried to get her to raise her hand. She already had eleven young ones at home. "I'll have to thank those women."

"A lot of them will be at the quilting bee on Saturday," Liddy said. "You could do it then. And bring Mandy along."

"I'd like that. Whose hope chest are we working to fill this time?"

"Beth Morgan is getting married next spring."

Emma took a drink of her coffee as she tried to put a face to the name. "Oh, she's an operator for the telephone company, isn't she?"

"That's right," Liddy confirmed.

"I don't remember seeing her with anyone. Who is she marrying?"

"She's going to Texas to marry a widower with two children," Liddy said. "She answered an advertisement in the paper."

"Really?" Mail-order brides weren't uncommon in the West, but Emma had never met anyone who actually was one. She'd seen the ads in the newspapers and been curious as to what kind of women answered them. She'd have to pay close attention on Saturday.

❧

Over the next week, Emma was able to express her appreciation to Nelda Harrison and Alma Burton when they came into her café. They both assured her that they would stand beside her. But the women who'd crossed the street rather than have any contact with Annie did the same thing now to Emma.

Emma thanked the Lord for women like Nelda and Alma. The others she prayed for—prayed that their hearts would change.

She was looking forward to the quilting bee on Saturday. She wasn't the best with a needle, and she was getting tired of making quilts for every engaged woman in town, but she did enjoy the chance to visit with women from her church. And she was curious to find out more about why Beth Morgan would agree to marry a man she'd never met.

The ladies at the quilting bee assured Emma that she would be a wonderful mother to Mandy. Their words encouraged her.

Mandy gleefully soaked in all the attention she received. Since the women taking turns holding the baby had much more experience raising children than she did, Emma began to relax and enjoy herself.

Beth Morgan was as sweet as she was pretty. Emma was glad when someone else had the nerve to ask her how she came to be engaged to a man she'd never met.

Beth smiled as she cut out a square of colorful fabric. "I told my friends I wondered what it would be like to correspond with one of those men who advertised in the paper, and they dared me to write to one. So I did. I never planned on falling in love with him."

The young woman giggled as she pulled a photograph out of her apron pocket. "This is a picture of him and his children. Aren't they lovely?" She handed the photo to the lady next to her to pass around. When it made its way to Emma, she was relieved to see that the man was clean-shaven and neatly groomed. His children appeared to be well taken care of.

"He appears to be nice, Beth," she said before handing the picture to Liddy. "I hope you'll be very happy."

"Thank you," Beth said.

"It occurs to me, Emma," said Harriet Howard, one of the older women in the group, "that might be the answer for you."

Emma scrunched her brow. "Answer to what?"

"Didn't Douglas Harper say that if you had a husband, there would be no problem with you keeping Annie's child?"

"Yes, but—"

"You could advertise for a mail-order groom!"

Emma chuckled along with the other women. "Why, Miss Harriet, I never heard of such an idea."

"If I were thirty years younger," Harriet said without glancing up from her stitching, "I might just put an advertisement in the paper myself."

Emma's amusement tapered off as she thought about the town council. "I can give Mandy a loving home all by myself. I don't need a man."

"Oh, I agree, Dear," Harriet said. "But it's a splendid idea, even if I do say so myself."

"Don't seem quite fair, does it?" Alma Burton said from the other side of the quilting frame. "That a man can order a bride, but a woman can't do the same for a groom."

"Fair or not, that's the way it is," Nelda Harrison said.

Emma sighed as she threaded a needle. Yes, that's the way it was.

☙

Matt hadn't seen Emma since the night of the town council meeting. He'd stopped by the café every night as usual. But yesterday she'd been shopping, and the day before that she was running errands. Now, according to Hallie and Ben, she was at some kind of ladies' meeting at church. Matt wondered if Emma was trying to avoid him.

He couldn't help but worry about her. He'd tried to talk to Sheriff Haynes about the situation with Harper. While the sheriff admitted he disagreed with what the town leaders were doing, they had to uphold the law. And if the town council voted to take the baby to Santa Fe, they would have to see that it was done.

Matt had heard plenty of grumbling around town. The men all liked gathering for coffee at Emma's. They were afraid raising a baby would be too much for her and she'd have to close down the café. There weren't many places in town where a man could get a decent meal and a cup of coffee, and none were as nice as Emma's, with the homey gingham table-cloths with matching curtains. The dining room in the Roswell Hotel was kind of uppity, and the hole-in-the-wall place next to the saloon down the street would get the men in mighty deep trouble if their womenfolk ever caught them there.

Not that there wasn't trouble now. Most of the wives, sisters, and mothers in town were hounding their men to pressure the council members into letting Emma keep the child. But together, those council members owned half the town. Harper himself had bought every spare parcel of land and property in Roswell, and it was difficult putting pressure on a man you owed money to.

Matt was beginning to question his own belief that Emma shouldn't have custody of Mandy. She wouldn't have to struggle to make a living like his mother had. Emma had a steady income, and she could hire people to help out. She loved the baby and would raise her well. Still, she'd been looking awful tired lately.

After finishing his afternoon rounds, he trudged back to the sheriff's office. He poured himself a cup of thick coffee, then took a seat outside, facing Emma's café. He propped his feet up on the horse rail and leaned back. He'd just watch her place until she got back.

Matt took a drink of the coffee and forced it down. He poured the rest out on the ground, then pulled his hat down to shade his eyes. It was getting near suppertime. Surely Emma would be back soon.

When he saw her emerge from the church on the corner and head toward the café, Matt was overwhelmed by a sense of relief. Hallie had told him the truth. She really was out.

When a loose board stopped the baby carriage, Emma fought to push the wheels over the uneven section. Matt rushed across the street to help. He lifted the carriage, baby and all, and set it down on the other side of the warped board. He tipped his hat. "Afternoon, Emma."

"Thank you for helping, Deputy," she responded with polite coolness.

"You're welcome." Matt pushed the carriage down the boardwalk. "She certainly seems to have enjoyed your outing."

Emma strolled beside him. "Yes, she did. We both did."

"You look good," Matt found himself saying. She seemed more rested than the last time he'd seen her. More relaxed.

"Thank you. I've been turning this whole situation over to the Lord. I'm also going to talk to a lawyer about legally adopting her."

Matt hoped the Lord would help Emma cope with whatever happened. He'd seen her church family reach out to her and believed they would support her, but he wasn't sure there was a lawyer in the county willing to go up against the town council.

"I can take it from here," Emma said.

Matt suddenly realized he'd pushed the baby carriage all the way to the café. "Let me help you over that hump in the threshold."

"Thank you," Emma said, opening the door and moving out of his way.

Once inside, she thanked him again and proceeded into the kitchen with Mandy.

"You're welcome," he called to her back. Matt strode out the door. Would he ever feel comfortable in Emma's presence again?

five

Mandy fell asleep early that evening. Emma kissed her forehead as she laid her on the bed. How precious this child had become to her in such a short time. *Dear God, please let there be a way for me to keep Mandy. Don't let that windbag Harper have his way.*

That man should have been run out of town years ago. Emma couldn't help but wonder what his motives were in wanting to take Mandy away.

She called the lawyer Cal and Liddy had recommended, and he agreed to see her on Monday. She would ask him if he thought she could legally adopt Mandy, even though she had no husband.

Emma sent Ben and Hallie home, telling them she could handle the few remaining customers. As she tidied up the empty tables, Emma thought about how thankful she was that she at least had the means to take care of herself and Mandy. Since the railroad came in, Roswell had become a bustling little town, and Emma's business had thrived. She'd even tucked away a fair amount in a savings account over the last few years, enough that she could start over somewhere else if worse came to worst. But Roswell was her home. She had no relatives elsewhere. All of her friends and her church family were here. This was where she wanted to raise Mandy.

After the last customer left, Emma poured herself a cup of coffee. She wished Liddy and Cal had a telephone so she could call her friend. She was feeling quite lonesome. Matt hadn't come in after his rounds for several days, at least not when she was there. Of course she shouldn't miss him. But she did.

Emma rose to start closing up when the bell above the door signaled a late customer. Her heart skittered as Matt walked in.

"Any coffee left?" he asked.

"Sure." Emma poured him a cup. "You finished with your rounds?"

Matt sat at the table she'd just vacated and put his hat on one of the extra chairs. "Yes. It's quiet tonight."

Emma brought the coffeepot to Matt's table and poured herself a second cup. "That's good, I guess."

"Hopefully, it'll stay that way awhile. Sheriff Haynes took the train to Eddy this morning to testify in a trial there." He blew on the hot liquid in his cup. "Said he'd probably be gone the better part of a week."

Emma sat across from Matt. But she didn't feel nearly as comfortable with him as she had a few weeks ago, and she found herself at a loss for what to say.

"Mandy asleep?"

"Yes." Emma smiled. "She had a very busy day. I took her to a quilting bee at church, and that little darlin' went from one woman's arms to another the whole time. Loved every minute of it, too."

"I bet she did. She's a charmer, that one."

Emma's heart warmed. "Yes, she is."

Matt cleared his throat. "How's your night going? Anything out of the ordinary?"

"No. Why?"

He rubbed his chin. "A few of the men in town are at odds

with their wives over your decision to keep Mandy."

"I see." Emma set her cup down so hard the coffee sloshed over the side. "And you've come to talk me into giving her up?"

"No, Emma. I just want to try to protect you."

"From what? A few husbands who aren't man enough to stand up to Harper?"

"Some of them are really angry, Emma. Their wives aren't even talking to them. But they owe Harper money, and they can't afford to make him mad."

"Well, I don't owe Harper anything. And I don't care if I make him mad." Emma rose from the table and picked up the two cups, even though his was still half full. "I'm not going to change my mind, Deputy. You can go tell *that* to all those complaining men, *including Councilman Harper!*"

Matt stood and settled his hat onto his head. "Emma, I—"

"Good night, Deputy. I need to close up."

"Emma Hanson!" The front door was flung wide by Jed Brewster. Emma knew little about the man, except that he owned a small farm outside of town. But she'd heard rumors that he drank too much. From the way he was weaving as he stood in the doorway, Emma suspected he'd spent far too long in one of the saloons down the street.

"I hope you're happy," he bellowed, pointing a wavering finger at Emma. "You've caused a lot of trouble between my missus and me."

He wobbled toward the center of the room, but Matt put a hand against his chest. "Stop right there, Jed. You have no right to come into Miss Emma's establishment carrying on like that."

Jed stopped, but his belligerent hollering continued. "She's cashing—I mean cooshing—*causing* problems for half the couples in town. Just 'cause she won't let a married couple have that baby."

"I don't recall any couples in town volunteering to take the baby," Matt said. "Now, you go on home, Jed."

The inebriated man glared at Emma. "Yes, well, I'd be taking that kid myself if I had anything to say about it."

Matt took Jed's arm. "Come on, it's time to go home. You need to sleep it off."

Jed jerked away. "No. I don't wanna go home. Laura's mad at me."

"I don't blame her. You smell like a still. How about I let you sleep in one of the cells tonight."

"I don't wanna go to jail."

"Well, you can come peaceable, or I can arrest you for causing a disturbance," Matt said, his hand hovering over the gun in his holster. "Your choice."

All the fight seemed to go out of Jed. His shoulders slumped and he let the deputy lead him to the door.

Matt glanced back at Emma. "Be sure and lock up behind us. And if you have any problems, just put through a call to me, you hear?"

"I will," Emma said as Matt nudged Jed out the door.

Much as she hated to admit it, Emma was awfully glad Matt had been there when Jed came in. She wasn't sure how she'd have handled things if she'd been alone.

Jed's wife, Laura, was a sweet lady, and Emma sure hated to think that she and Jed were having trouble because of her. She didn't want to cause problems for any of the couples in town. But she couldn't let Mandy go. She just couldn't.

Emma climbed the stairs and checked on the baby. How precious she was with her eyes closed, breathing so peacefully.

Emma twisted a little curl around her finger and felt its softness. *Oh, Annie. How beautiful she is. I wish you were still here for her. But I promised you I'd take her, and I'll do my best to keep that promise. With God's help she'll become the woman you would wish her to be.*

৵

After church and then dinner at Cal and Liddy's, Emma spent some time resting and playing with Mandy.

The café was busier the next morning than it had ever been on a Monday. It seemed half the town showed up for breakfast or brunch. And not just her regular customers. Complete strangers came in, too. Gossip about the council meeting the week before must have spread to all the farms and ranches on the outskirts of town.

Emma couldn't break away from the rush to see Cal and Liddy's lawyer until midafternoon. When she did speak to him, he wasn't as reassuring as she'd hoped. He was going out of town the next day to represent a client at a trial, and he wasn't sure how long he would be gone. So he couldn't do anything right away, he said, even if there was anything that could be done. Still, he promised to check into the situation when he returned.

Emma felt certain the town council would take things into their own hands before the lawyer got back. She left his office with a heavy heart, but as she walked back to the café, she reminded herself to leave the situation in God's hands. He would take care of everything.

When Emma opened the door to the café, she stopped in shock. The place was packed, every table occupied. But even stranger, all the men were seated on one side of the room, while their wives sat at tables on the opposite side. And each group was grumbling about the other.

The men barely glanced up when Emma entered, but the women surrounded her, gushing about how much they admired her for taking Mandy in. Emma was tempted to hightail it out of there, leaving the café in Ben and Hallie's hands.

"Afternoon, Emma."

She turned and saw Matt standing in the doorway. "Deputy."

He scanned the crowded room as the women resumed their seats and their mumbling. "I wondered why the streets seemed so deserted." He grinned. "Any problems?"

So far, none of the men looked like they were going to attack her. "Not yet."

Matt raised an eyebrow. "The air is a bit thick in here today, isn't it?"

Emma chuckled.

"That's a nice sound to hear again."

Emma shrugged. "Might as well laugh. Crying won't help anything."

"Deputy Carmichael is relieving me in about an hour. I'll come back then for supper."

"I'm sure I'll be fine, Deputy. No need for you to work overtime."

Matt raised an eyebrow and took his time looking around the room before heading to the door. "I'll be back."

❧

After supper the crowd started to thin out. Emma breathed a sigh of relief. She felt utterly exhausted.

She padded into the kitchen, where Ben was finishing the dishes. Hallie came downstairs with a pajama-clad Mandy in her arms. When Emma took the baby, Mandy cuddled close. "Em-mama!"

Emma breathed in the fresh scents of lye soap and talcum powder. "You smell so sweet, Mandy baby. I haven't seen enough of you today."

"Sure was extra busy, wasn't it?" Ben said, putting away the roasting pan. "What's going on?"

Emma sat at the kitchen table, adjusted the baby on her lap, and took a sip of the hot tea Hallie set in front of her. "It seems the town is divided on whether I should keep Mandy or give her up. Mostly, men against the women."

"Oh, that's not right," Hallie said, taking a seat across from Emma.

"No, it's not." Emma kissed Mandy on the top of the head. "But I don't know what to do about it."

"Not much you can do, Miss Emma," Ben said. "The way I see it, them husbands and wives are just gonna have to agree to disagree."

"Maybe once they get home, they'll talk it over." Emma rubbed her chin over the baby's soft hair.

The bell above the front door jingled and Hallie peeked around the kitchen door. "I wouldn't count on that if I were you. A passel of men just came in. Want I should go take their orders?"

"No, thank you, Hallie." Emma rose, settled Mandy on her hip, and bustled out to the dining room.

"What can I get you fellows?" she asked the eight men who stood at the counter.

"We ain't here to eat," Homer Williams said. "We come here to try to talk some sense into you." He pointed at Mandy. "Why, just look at you. Trying to take care of a young'un and run a business at the same time. It's too much for one woman to do; can't you see that?"

"No, Homer, I can't. I'm taking care of everything just fine. And I do have help." She motioned for Hallie to come into the dining room. Then she handed Mandy to her and asked her to take the baby back to the kitchen.

"I refuse to discuss the subject of giving up Mandy," Emma said firmly. "Now, what can I get for you gentlemen? Mrs. McAllister brought in some real nice peach pies this morning."

"We're here for a meal," Harold Ferguson said. "Beatrice says she's not feeling up to cooking tonight."

"Nelda said the same thing," Jim Harrison said, glaring at Emma. "Said she wasn't much hungry. Well, no wonder, after all that tea and cake she ate here this afternoon."

The others started grumbling about their wives, too. Emma was tempted to tell them to take their business elsewhere, but these men were regulars, and she felt a little sorry for them. There wasn't much she could do, but she could at least feed them.

"The roast chicken is mighty tasty tonight. Any takers?"

Five of the men took seats at a couple of adjoining tables. The rest filed out the door, still grumbling.

Emma began to relax. "So, that's five plates of roast chicken?"

"Make it six."

Emma spun around and saw Matt right behind her. He must have come in through the back door off the kitchen.

"You handled that very well," he whispered as he followed her to the kitchen.

Emma felt warmth creep into her cheeks. "Thank you." Her heart did its familiar somersault, and she wondered how long he'd been there. She tried not to show how glad she was that he'd come back like he said he would. With him in the café, maybe the rest of the night would pass calmly.

Emma dished out the plates of roast chicken, and the men ate their meals in relative quiet. Matt sat alone at the table next to theirs.

After the others left, he ordered dessert. Apparently, he intended to stay until she closed, and much as she hated to admit it, Emma felt safer with him there.

She poured Matt a second cup of coffee and sat across from him. "Thank you, Deputy."

"For what?"

He wasn't going to make it easy on her, and she couldn't really blame him. "For checking on me and Mandy, making sure we are all right, protecting us from the men of this town. . . even though you agree with them."

Matt set down his cup. "Emma, I'm not like those men."

"But you said yourself that Mandy would be better off with a married couple."

"And I still believe that."

Emma pushed herself away from the table and started clearing the one behind her. "You're off duty, aren't you? There's no reason for you to spend your time off making sure my night goes well. I'll just close early tonight."

"Emma, I don't mind—"

"I know." She shot him a withering glare. "But I do."

Matt stood. "I understand."

"Besides, I—" Emma caught herself before she told him she hadn't spent enough time with Mandy. That bit of knowledge certainly wouldn't make him change his mind about her situation. "I have a lot to do to get ready for tomorrow."

"I'll let you get to work, then." Matt paid for his meal, and Emma followed him to the door. "Tell Ben the food was delicious as always."

"I will."

"Good night, Emma."

Her heart twisted at the dejected expression in his eyes. She wondered if he felt as distressed as she did. He seemed about to say something more, but then he turned and walked out the door.

"Good night." She locked the door, flipped over the CLOSED sign, and pulled down the shade. This was one day she was glad to be done with.

six

The next few days passed much the same for Emma. She was extremely busy, with customers who were more than a little grumpy. . .all because she wanted to keep a promise.

When Liddy came in with her baked goods, she stared with raised eyebrows at the fifteen tables in Emma's café, all filled with people. "Appears you could use a little extra help."

Emma gladly accepted her offer. The two of them and Hallie had their hands full taking care of the crowd. Poor Ben worked triple-time to keep up with all the cooking.

Emma took orders with Mandy hoisted on her hip. The baby chortled at all the customers who talked to her and cooed at her.

At midafternoon, when the crowd finally left, Liddy let out a long sigh. "My goodness, Em! I should have brought more pies."

"If you had a telephone, I'd have called to ask you to bring more."

"Actually," Liddy said, "the telephone company has just started putting lines up out our way. As soon as they can hook us up, you'll be able to call me." She followed Emma into the kitchen with an armload of dirty dishes. "I wouldn't be surprised if every single person in town ate lunch here today."

"I think the only person I haven't seen lately is Harper," Emma said.

Liddy shivered. "Just the thought of that man makes my skin crawl."

Emma settled Mandy in her special corner of the kitchen. "I keep waiting for him to barge in here and take Mandy and deliver her to Santa Fe personally."

"Let him try," Ben said. "He'd have to get through me first."

"And me second," Hallie added. "We ain't gonna let him take this baby, Miss Emma."

"Bless you all," Emma said, grateful to God for such faithful friends. "But I think the sheriff's deputy is watching this place pretty closely. I sure am thankful we're right across the street from their office."

She looked at the new telephone on the wall. So far, she'd only used it for calls to the doctor. . .to check on Annie before she died. Still, she was glad she'd had it installed. "Even though my newfangled telephone doesn't get much use, it's comforting to know I can call the sheriff's office if I need to."

Hallie and Ben started on the dishes while Emma and Liddy straightened up out front. As Emma brought an armful of plates into the kitchen, she heard the distinctive peal of the telephone. It made one long and two short sounds to alert her that someone was trying to reach her. She set down the plates and crossed the room to the shiny wooden box hanging on the wall. She lifted the black earpiece from its hook and spoke into the cone-shaped mouthpiece. "Yes?" she said, both excited about receiving her first call and nervous about what the news might be.

"Miss Emma?" The woman's voice sounded soft and hesitant.

"Yes. Who is this?"

"It's Laura Brewster. I–I just wanted to apologize for my husband's outburst the other night. I hope you won't charge him with causing a disturbance in your café. When I got him out of jail, Deputy Johnson said you could, if you were of a mind to. But he's sobered up and he's real sorry."

Emma hadn't even thought about pressing charges against Jed. Matt had probably just said that to try to scare Jed into behaving himself. *He's not much of a man to let his wife apologize for him,* she thought as she heard Laura sobbing on the other end of the line.

"Don't cry, Laura. If Jed doesn't give me any more trouble, there's no need for me to charge him with anything."

"You mean it, Miss Hanson?" Laura sniffled. "Oh, thank you so much. I promise he'll act like a gentleman from now on."

Emma heard a jostling sound, then a sudden clunk. "Laura?"

"She's disconnected on her end, Emma," a familiar voice said.

"Beth? Is that you?"

"Yes, it is. Mrs. Brewster must have said all she wanted to."

"I guess so," Emma said, amazed at this new technology.

"Want I should ring her line?" Beth asked.

"No, thank you."

"All right. Have a good afternoon."

Emma placed the earpiece back on its hook and turned to the curious faces watching her from the table.

"What was that all about?" Liddy asked with a furrowed brow.

"Jed Brewster had too much to drink the other night, and he came in here to tell me I should give Mandy up."

"Manny up," the baby said from her corner. She grinned when the adults chuckled. "I hungy," she said, pulling herself up against the makeshift fence in the play area.

"I creamed her some potatoes just a few minutes ago, Miss Emma," Ben said. "She likes them that way."

Emma picked Mandy up and gave her a hug before settling

her in her high chair. "Here you go, Sweetie; let's get you some food."

"I'd better get on home and make sure my family has something to eat," Liddy said. She took her bonnet off the hook. "You be sure and lock up tight. Jed might not be the only one trying to cause problems for you. Wouldn't surprise me a bit if he was working for old Harper."

"That thought crossed my mind, too. Hopefully his wife has more influence on him than Harper does."

Liddy kissed the top of Mandy's head on her way out the back door. "I'm going to check with the telephone company to see when they think they'll be ready to install our telephone. It would be nice to be able to find out how you and Mandy are doing when I can't get to town."

"You just can't stand it because I have a telephone and you don't," Emma teased.

Liddy laughed. "Something like that. Actually, living out where we do, it'd be nice to know we could get hold of the sheriff's office or the doctor if we needed to. But what I'd *really* like is an icebox like you have."

"I am blessed, that's for sure," Emma said.

"So am I. But I do envy you sometimes."

"And I've envied you for your wonderful family."

"But now you have Mandy."

Emma choked back a sob. "I just hope I can keep her."

"Don't worry," Liddy said. "God will make sure everything comes out right."

"That's what I'm counting on."

≈

That evening, Emma had Ben roast an extra cut of beef, preparing for the next rush. But dinnertime came and went, and almost no one showed up. It appeared the town was now staging a boycott of her place.

Emma sent Hallie home early and told Ben to put the meat in the icebox.

"It'll make a fine stew tomorrow." Ben took the beef out of the roasting pan, placed it on a wooden board, and cut it into stew-sized chunks.

Emma smiled. "It'll be our special of the day." As she started toward the front door to flip the OPEN sign around to CLOSED, Matt walked in.

"Anything left to eat?" he asked, hanging his Stetson on the hook.

"If you'd like roast beef, we have plenty."

"That'd be just fine." Matt took a seat at his regular table. "Slow night?"

"Very."

"You want I should fix a plate for the deputy, Miss Emma?" Ben asked from the kitchen door.

"Give the deputy a large portion, Ben. It'll be that much less to try to fit in the icebox."

Ben chuckled as he stepped back into the kitchen.

Emma poured Matt a cup of coffee. "I've only had a handful of customers this evening."

"Well, you had a lot in here for dinner. Maybe no one is hungry."

Emma shrugged. "Maybe."

Ben came in carrying a plate piled high with roast beef, carrots, potatoes, and gravy and set it in front of Matt. "Hope you enjoy it."

"I'm sure I will. Thank you."

Ben returned to the kitchen, and Matt looked up at Emma.

"Why don't you sit a spell while I eat?"

"Might as well." Emma poured herself a cup of coffee and sat across from him. She took a sip. "I'm thinking of changing my hours."

"Oh?" Matt cut into the roast and forked a piece of meat into his mouth.

"I thought I might close for a few hours in the afternoon, then open back up for suppertime. That would give Ben and Hallie a break, too."

Matt swallowed his bite. "And it would give you more time with Mandy."

"Yes, it would."

"I think it's a great idea." Matt stabbed another piece of beef.

"I thought so, even before I started taking care of Mandy. But now I'm concerned that the town council could somehow use that against me, saying that raising a baby and running a business is too much for me."

Matt stared at her, his loaded fork in midair. "Is it?"

"No," Emma said sharply, tired of his incessant questioning of her ability to take care of Mandy and the café. "I guess I forgot who I was talking to. Why can't I remember that you're not on my side in this?"

"Emma, you're wrong about that. I just remember my mother trying to raise us alone—"

"And what if someone had decided to take you and your brothers away from your mother just because she was a widow?" Emma grabbed Matt's plate. "The meal is on me, Deputy. It's closing time."

She swung around and stormed into the kitchen.

❧

Matt sat at the table with a forkful of beef partway to his

mouth. He took the bite, but somehow it didn't taste near as good as the rest of the meal had.

Ben came though the kitchen door. "You need anything else, Deputy? Miss Emma took Mandy upstairs for the night and asked me to close up for her."

Matt took a last swallow from his cup. "No, thanks, Ben. I seem to have lost my appetite." He paid Ben for his meal.

Ben put the cash in the moneybox. "Miss Emma's had a rough week."

"Yes, she has," Matt said, putting on his hat. "But I wish she hadn't flown off like that. I wanted to let her know I'm going to be out of town for several days. I've got to take a prisoner to Lincoln."

"I'll tell her, Deputy."

Matt thanked Ben and made his way to the door. Then he turned back. "You watch out for her, you hear?"

"Oh, I will."

Matt clapped Ben on the shoulder. "I'll sleep better knowing you'll be keeping an eye on things."

"You have a safe trip," Ben said.

&

Emma came back downstairs to help Ben close up as soon as she was sure Matt had left. She shouldn't have been so rude to him. The way she'd practically forced him out of the café certainly wasn't very Christlike. Emma felt even worse when Ben told her Matt was going out of town for a few days.

"Don't you worry none about anythin' while Deputy Matt is gone," Ben said. "I promised to look after you and the baby."

"Thank you, Ben. And the Lord is going to take care of us all."

"Yes'm, He is."

They quietly cleaned up the kitchen and made preparations for the next day. After Ben went home for the night, Emma locked up. But she wasn't quite ready to call it a night. She brewed herself a cup of tea and prayed for forgiveness in treating Matt so badly.

❧

Deputy Carmichael began taking all his meals at the café. Emma figured Matt must have asked him to keep an eye on her while he was gone. The young deputy was handsome and charming, if a bit shy. Emma was sure most of the unattached gals in Chaves County were scheming to change his single status.

Business returned to normal, for which Emma was grateful. She'd learned in the last few days that there was indeed such a thing as being too busy.

She was still contemplating the possibility of closing between three and five in the afternoon. That was when some of the ladies came in for afternoon tea, and Emma did feel a certain loyalty to them. But they could just as easily meet at the Roswell Hotel's dining room at that time of day.

That afternoon Beth Morgan, Myrtle Bradshaw, and several other ladies from church came in for tea.

"How is that little darling doing?" the doctor's wife asked.

Like a proud mother, Emma answered, "Growing every day and beginning to get into things. Would you like to see her?"

"We'd love to." Beth grinned.

Emma carried Mandy out front, and the little girl flew straight into Myrtle's arms. After getting a big hug, she went to each of the others at the table, securing her place in everyone's hearts.

"You know," Myrtle said, "anytime you need to run an errand and want someone to watch this pretty little thing, you just let me know."

"Me, too," Beth added. "At least, until I get married."

"How are your wedding preparations going?" Emma asked as she set cream and sugar on the table.

"Just wonderful. As a matter of fact, there's been a change in plans. He's coming here! He decided he wants to come out West to settle down."

"That's terrific, Beth." Emma was truly happy for her.

Mandy lunged from Opal Barber's arms into Emma's and laid her head on Emma's shoulder.

"She's quite attached to you, isn't she?" Beth asked.

"And well she should be," Myrtle said. "She loved Emma even before Annie passed away. I'll never forget the night you came and got her, Emma. She went straight to you and settled right down. She'd been fussy for me up until then."

"It'll be a shame if Harper gets his way and takes her away from you," Mrs. Barber said. Then she clamped a hand over her mouth.

"That would be a shame," Emma said, trying to put Mrs. Barber's mind at ease. "But I'm trusting in the Lord for that not to happen. I know He'll make a way for me to keep her."

"I wouldn't count on that, Miss Emma," a deep voice said. Emma swung around and saw Douglas Harper standing right behind her. "At least not unless you follow Miss Morgan's example and answer one of those advertisements for a husband." He chuckled.

Emma shook from head to foot. She wanted to tell that horrible man to get out of her establishment immediately, but she knew that wouldn't help her cause. She tamped down her anger and frustration and tried to speak calmly. "Did you come for afternoon tea, Councilman?"

"No, thank you. I just came to let you know that the folks in Santa Fe will be calling in a week or so with their final decision." He tipped his hat to the ladies at the table and sauntered out the door.

Emma sank into the nearest chair.

Myrtle poured Emma a cup of tea from the pot on the table. "That man makes chills run down my spine."

"What is it about him that has half the men in this town afraid to stand up to him?" Opal asked.

"At least *our* husbands don't agree with him," Myrtle said. She patted Emma's hand. "You can rest assured of that."

Emma smiled at the doctor's wife. "It does my heart good to know that."

"And hardly any woman in town is on Harper's side in this," Beth added, "except for those few who look down on a child from an unknown background. Everyone in our ladies' group is praying about it."

"I appreciate that more than I can say. I know God is listening."

"Still and all," Opal said, "it's too bad you don't have a husband. If you did, none of this would be a problem."

seven

Emma tossed and turned most of the night. She tried to tell herself that the town council must have changed their minds about letting her keep Mandy. But from the snippets of conversation she'd overheard from her customers, Harper seemed more determined than ever to try to take the child away from her.

Lord, please show me what You want me to do. She needed to stop worrying and truly leave things in God's hands. He had a plan. She just didn't know what it was yet.

Unable to get back to sleep, Emma trudged downstairs, hoping the "peace of God, which passeth all understanding" would overtake her in the still of the morning. While she was stoking the stove, she thought about Beth Morgan and her mail-order husband.

Emma snorted. "I certainly wouldn't want to answer an advertisement from a man I don't even know," she said out loud. "He'd probably want me to leave my business and move to where he lived." Beth's man had apparently decided to join her, but that wasn't the norm.

Then she recalled Harriet Howard's amusing comment about advertising for a mail-order groom. Emma chuckled to herself. Why not? Just because it had never been done didn't mean it couldn't be. That way, the woman could choose which letters to answer and respond only to the men who seemed to suit her.

Emma shook her head. She could never do that. She'd be

the laughingstock of the town.

She poured herself a cup of tea and sat at the table. With a smirk tugging at her lips, she wondered what steps she'd take if she were to place such an advertisement. Lincoln and Eddy both had local papers, as did several towns in between. If she only advertised locally, she wouldn't be asking anyone to move terribly far from where he lived. And she could meet the applicants in person before she committed to one of them. Emma began to tingle with excitement as she considered exactly how she would word such an advertisement. . .if she were to write one. After mulling it over for a few moments, she dug a pen and a pad of paper from the stationery box she kept on a shelf by the staircase and jotted down some ideas.

She scratched out and rewrote several times, then finally settled on a paragraph she was sure would attract the right kind of man. . .if there were such a thing. As she read it over and over, she imagined men of strong moral fiber and firm Christian faith seeing this advertisement, believing the Lord Himself had led them straight to her—Emma Hanson of Roswell, New Mexico.

"You know, this could work," she told herself. If it didn't, she had nothing to lose. But if it did. . .she would have a husband. Mandy would have a father. And Harper wouldn't have a leg to stand on!

Emma rewrote the advertisement on a fresh scrap of paper, then copied it several times for the various newspapers she'd put it in. If she could get to the bank and have them draw payment drafts that morning, she could get the envelopes on the afternoon train to Hagerman and Eddy, and by stage to Lincoln and the smaller towns.

After closing the last envelope, she heard Mandy calling for

Em-mama. Emma scampered up the stairs. She took the little girl out of her bed and swung her around, eliciting peals of laughter from the child.

"Oh, sweet Mandy. We're going to find you a daddy!"

After dressing herself and the baby, she hurried back downstairs and stuffed the letters into her apron pocket. She'd mail them as soon as business slowed down after breakfast.

If Ben was surprised to find her humming as she mixed the bread dough and set it to rise, he didn't say anything. But when Liddy arrived with her pie delivery, she pulled Emma to the side right away. "What's up with you?"

"Why, whatever do you mean?" Emma asked playfully.

"You're in a terribly good mood today. Did Harper pull up stakes and move away?"

Emma laughed. "I wish." Then, feeling that she had to tell *someone,* she decided to confide in her best friend. "I may have found a way to thwart his plans, though."

"Really? What is it?"

"I'm going to take Harriet's advice."

"Harriet?" Liddy appeared puzzled for a few moments. Then her mouth fell open. "Don't tell me you're thinking about advertising for a husband!"

Emma grinned. "I'm only going to put ads in the Lincoln and Chaves County papers, not the Roswell papers." She patted her apron pocket. "I plan on mailing these as soon as the breakfast rush is over."

Liddy put her hand over her mouth. "Oh, Em. Are you sure you want to do this?"

"According to the town council, I need a husband." She grinned. "Can you see Harper's face when I tell him that I found one?"

Liddy laughed. "I'll watch the café while you go mail those if you like."

I think I'll take you up on that offer."

Emma made sure the customers who'd already placed their orders were served, then put Mandy into her carriage and walked out the door.

She strolled down the boardwalk, enjoying the sunshine. Her first stop was the bank. After getting the appropriate payment drafts for the different newspapers, she tucked each draft into its corresponding envelope. When she arrived at the postmaster's office, she handed Mr. Marley her stack. She held her breath while he gave them a once-over.

"You putting an advertisement in these papers, Miss Emma?"

"Yes," Emma answered without offering more information.

Mr. Marley nodded. "I don't blame you. It's certainly the way to go these days."

Emma felt heat rise in her face. Surely he didn't know what she was advertising for. "I hope so."

"My sister owns a boardinghouse up in Amarillo, and since she started advertising in the papers, she's seen a big increase in her business."

Emma cleared her throat. "That's wonderful."

"Hopefully, that'll happen for you. Although your café seems to be doing real well. I guess it don't hurt none to make sure." He dropped her envelopes onto the various stacks of letters behind him. "You have a pleasant day, Miss Emma." He leaned over the counter and grinned at Mandy. "And you, too, little girl."

When Emma returned to the café, she found Liddy taking orders as if she'd been doing it all her life. When she noticed Cal there refilling coffee cups, she said, "I'm sorry, Liddy.

Did it get so busy you needed extra help?"

Liddy laughed. "No. I just forgot I was supposed to meet Cal at the Joyce Pruit store today. When I didn't show up, he came to find me."

"I was afraid she'd run away from home," Cal teased.

"He did track mud on my clean floor last night." Liddy winked at Emma.

"I promise I'll make it up to you," Cal said.

"I know you will."

Emma thanked them for their help, then watched them head for Joyce Pruit. Cal cupped a hand on Liddy's elbow, helping her along the uneven boardwalk. His head dipped close to hers, listening to what she was saying. Emma hoped she would have that kind of relationship with a husband one day—no matter how they might meet.

Emma hugged her secret to herself for the rest of the day. When she heard the whistle of the afternoon train, her stomach fluttered in excitement. Her ads were on their way. How long would it take before they came out in the papers? And how long would it be before she received her first response?

Hopeful excitement carried her through the rest of the day, and as she put Mandy to bed for the night, she felt satisfied that she was doing all she could do to keep her. Just before she dozed off, she wondered what Matt would have to say about her advertisement.

❧

Emma opened her eyes the next morning with a smile, listening to Mandy's soft breathing. She stretched leisurely, then suddenly remembered the ads. She sat straight up in bed, a wave of panic washing over her, making her wonder if she was going to be sick to her stomach.

What had she done? What was she thinking? Oh, why hadn't Liddy stopped her? Struggling for breath, she threw off the covers and gathered her clothes for the day. Maybe the letters hadn't gone out yet. Perhaps there was some kind of remorse rule about mail—that the postmaster had to hold all letters for a day before sending them on. Emma snorted. And maybe a prince would answer her advertisement! She put her hand on her chest and forced herself to take a deep breath.

Emma pulled on her stockings and cinched herself into her corset. *What kind of man would answer an advertisement like that anyway?* She tucked her shirtwaist between her petticoat and her skirt. *And how desperate will he think I am?*

Emma fell to her knees beside the bed. *Oh, dear Lord, please forgive me. I took things into my own hands instead of waiting on You. I'm so sorry.*

Mandy cried out, and Emma went to her bed. As she picked up the child and cuddled her, she realized that now she *had* to trust in the Lord to make everything all right. She certainly didn't know how to. She just hoped He understood.

Emma felt quite meek for the next few days. She went from praying that no one would answer the advertisement to praying that the right man would. In church on Sunday, she felt even more humbled when the sermon was about trusting in God. She acknowledged to the Lord, and herself, that she hadn't trusted enough. She prayed for greater faith that God would cause everything to work out for His glory.

After Sunday dinner, Cal took the children outside to check on the livestock while Emma and Liddy cleaned up the kitchen.

"What's wrong, Em?" Liddy asked. "Are you having second thoughts about the ads?"

Emma shrugged. "Am I that transparent?"

"Well, you aren't exactly humming today." Liddy poured coffee and motioned for Emma to sit down.

Emma sank into the chair across from her friend. "How could I have thought that was the answer? What would make me do such a silly thing?"

"I don't think it was silly. If you find the right man for you and Mandy this way, it will have turned into a blessing."

Emma took a sip of her coffee, then put her cup down, twirling it around on its saucer. "And what if I meet the wrong man?"

"You don't have to answer any of the letters, you know."

Emma peered up at Liddy and grinned. "You're right. I forgot about that."

"That's why you put the advertisement in the paper. . .so you could have a choice. Just leave it in God's hands."

"Oh, I know He's the only One who can make things come out right. I have to remind myself that He's in control and quit trying to take it back from Him."

"We all have to remind ourselves of that. But when we do hand it over to Him, He turns everything to good in a way we never could. Remember how the Lord got Cal and me together? He even used you to get us started. Why, if you hadn't been blabbing your mouth about me to Cal—"

"That's the thanks I get for helping you two get together?" The women enjoyed a welcome laugh.

By the time she and Mandy got back home, Emma felt at peace. She still didn't know what to do, but she was convinced that God did.

๛

After a cold supper, Matt tied his prisoner's hands and feet to a tree for the night. Horse thief Jack Carlson wasn't escaping on his watch if he could help it.

Matt threw a pile of sticks on the fire. The air was cooler up here in the foothills than down in Roswell.

"You ain't gonna live 'til morning," Carlson snarled. "My brother'll be here before dawn, so you better say your prayers."

Matt tried to ignore the man's taunts. Although most of his prisoner's cronies were in various jails across the territory, Jack's brother, Hank, wasn't. Matt had been on the lookout for Carlson's brother all day.

But the trip had been uneventful thus far. Matt uttered a prayer of thankfulness under his breath. Still, he wasn't going to let his guard down.

Leaning back against a nearby tree where he had a good view of the campsite, Matt kept a close eye on his prisoner until the man seemed to fall asleep. Then his thoughts wandered to Emma.

He couldn't stop thinking about what she'd said the night before he left. What if someone had decided his mother shouldn't be raising him and his brothers, and tried to send them away? She would have fought with everything in her to keep her children, just as Emma was fighting now.

Emma and Mandy belonged together. He wished they belonged to him—that he could be both a family man and a lawman. Perhaps it was possible. After all, his duties weren't terribly dangerous. Most of the time he simply wandered up and down the streets of Roswell, making sure everything was quiet. . .which it usually was. The worst scrapes he'd encountered on the job were an occasional drifter cheating at cards or a drunken cowboy starting a fistfight.

For the first time, Matt began to seriously consider what it would be like to be married to Emma Hanson, to help her raise little Mandy. His heart yearned to make those two his family.

His thoughts were disturbed by a soft shuffling sound. Matt squinted at Carlson. The prisoner appeared to still be asleep. Telling himself it was probably just an animal, Matt shifted his position to try to get comfortable on the hard ground. He'd sure be glad to have this trip over with and get back to Roswell.

He heard a snap, as if someone had stepped on a twig. Every muscle in Matt's body tensed. It might not be anything more than a deer, but he couldn't be sure. He allowed his head to slump down, pretending he'd fallen asleep, but kept his eyes slightly open. He faked a small snore. Then, as silently as he could, he slipped the Colt .44 out of his holster and eased back the hammer.

Matt heard a crackle that sounded like leaves being crushed. He stayed perfectly still, his forefinger on the trigger.

Through the slits of his half-shut eyes, Matt saw on the ground a shadow creeping up from behind the tree he leaned against. The prisoner's eyes opened. Jack glanced at Matt; then his gaze shifted to a spot over Matt's shoulder.

With muffled whispering, a lone figure came around the tree Matt was leaning against and crept over to Jack. Matt barely breathed. The figure knelt in front of Carlson and began to untie his feet.

Matt aimed his pistol at the two men. "I'd stop right there if I was you," he said in his most menacing voice.

The figure turned, pulled a gun, and fired in one smooth motion. Hearing the *zing* of a bullet fly by his ear, Matt scrambled behind the tree. He shot at the dark figure. With a scream, the man grabbed his right forearm with his left hand. His gun flew into the air and landed in the dirt. The figure fell over, moaning with pain.

"You killed my brother!" Jack yelled.

"No, he didn't," Hank cried, holding the bloody arm close to his body. "But he might as well have. He got my shooting hand!"

Matt crept out into the open, his gun raised. "You're lucky that's all I aimed for."

Never taking his eyes off the two men, Matt gathered Hank's gun from the dirt, pulled more rope out of his saddlebag, and marched his new prisoner to a tree a few feet away from the first one. Hank hollered like a wolf when Matt pressed his injured arm against the tree trunk and wrapped the rope around his wrists.

"You just gonna let him bleed to death?" Jack asked.

Matt tightened the rope. "He'll be taken care of soon enough."

Once both of the men were secured, facing in opposite directions, Matt checked Hank's hand. The bullet had gone straight through the palm, and although there was a lot of bleeding, it seemed to be a clean wound. Matt dug through his saddlebag, but found nothing that could be used as a bandage. He grabbed a clean shirt. After ripping it into pieces, Matt wrapped the man's hand as best he could. It would do until they got to Lincoln.

Matt didn't sleep a wink all night. When he wasn't thinking about his sudden brush with death, his thoughts returned to Emma. How foolish he'd been to entertain the idea of marrying her. Why, just moments ago he could have been shot dead. His job might be uneventful most of the time, but it would only take one bullet to make Emma a widow and Mandy fatherless again.

At first light, Matt found Hank's horse grazing near his own and the one he'd used to transport Jack. He untied the two men and retied them to the saddles, stringing the horses together.

❧

Matt emerged from the Lincoln County sheriff's office, twisting his neck to get the kinks out. He'd brought Jack Carlson in safe and sound.

Sheriff Miller was pleased as punch that Matt had Hank in custody, too. Together, the two brothers had four outstanding warrants for their arrest. Their futures would be in the hands of a judge and jury soon.

Matt swung back into the saddle and headed down the street to the Lincoln Hotel. It was a small establishment, but it did have a dining room. He'd wash some of the dust off himself, enjoy a good meal, then get some much-needed sleep.

The warm bath eased his aches somewhat, but down in the dining room, after chewing on the toughest piece of meat he'd ever eaten and tasting one bite of lumpy mashed potatoes, he determined that Emma and Ben could out-cook whoever was in this kitchen.

Taking a last swallow of bad coffee, Matt admitted to himself that he didn't just miss the cooking. He missed the company at the café. He sure hoped everything was quiet in Roswell, and that no one else had given Emma a hard time while he was gone.

Matt wondered why Harper was so determined to place Mandy in an orphanage. He promised himself to look into that when he got home, but at the moment he was too tired to figure it all out. He headed upstairs to his room, yawning with every step.

❧

By Monday, Emma figured her advertisement had been placed in at least a few of the local papers, but she realized it would be several days before she received any replies. Still, she began checking her post office box on Tuesday and felt relieved when she found nothing there.

Although her café kept her busy, things seemed pretty quiet around town. The sheriff was back, and he and Deputy Carmichael seemed to take turns eating meals with Emma. She wondered when Matt would be back but didn't want to ask anyone. Although she missed him, she convinced herself that it was better that he was gone. She needed to accept, once and for all, that there was no future for her and Matthew Johnson.

Still, she did feel the need to apologize to him for being so rude the night before he left. He couldn't help how he felt.

Over the next several days, Emma checked the post office after each stage and train delivery. No replies to her advertisement appeared, and she didn't know whether to be relieved or disappointed.

She prayed for patience as she pushed Mandy's baby carriage back to the café. If a husband was in God's plan for her, He would see to it that the right man answered her advertisement— or that she would meet him in a more conventional manner—in His way and in His time.

❧

After sleeping most of the day, Matt was ready to head back to Roswell. He bounded down the stairs and paid his bill, then braved the dining room for breakfast. Surely no one could ruin bacon and eggs. He placed his order and picked up a newspaper off the unoccupied table beside him.

First he caught up on the local news of Lincoln, then he scanned the Help Wanted section. A local rancher was searching for more hands. The hotel needed a new cook. *That's an understatement.*

The rotund waitress plunked down a coffee cup in front of him. He took a sip as he scanned the Personals. A young boy was searching for his dog. A church social was planned for the following week. Matt choked on his coffee when he read the next advertisement.

Husband wanted. Good Christian woman who runs her own business is looking for an upright, sober, faithful Christian man. Must like children. Please reply to Emma Hanson, Box 789, Roswell, Chaves County, New Mexico Territory.

When he finally got his coughing spell under control, Matt read the advertisement again. Guilt washed over him. What had Harper forced her into? He knew Emma wouldn't give up Mandy without a fight, but this? She could have her pick of men. As Matt read the advertisement one more time, a cold fear gripped him. What was Emma letting herself in for? Any type of man could answer that advertisement. And there were all types out there.

He threw coins onto the table to pay for the breakfast he no longer wanted, then grabbed his saddlebags and headed for the livery stable. He had to get back to Roswell as soon as possible—to warn Emma. . .and *try* to talk some sense into her!

eight

Emma took the envelope from Mr. Marley with trembling fingers. She went outside to open it, then quickly read the first reply to her advertisement. She didn't know whether to laugh or cry. The letter didn't indicate how old the man was, but he wrote that he'd outlived two wives and had ten children and eight grandchildren. He assured her he was "good for at least ten more years" and that he was a God-fearing man. Emma's innate sense of humor rescued her from disappointment. She tore up the letter and stuffed the pieces into her pocket.

It could be worse, she told herself as she strolled back to the café. *The letter might have been from a criminal.* She shivered just thinking about that.

"Em-mama!" Mandy greeted her with uplifted arms when she entered the café. Emma lifted the baby as Mandy added, "I luz you."

Emma hugged the child close. "I love you, too, my Mandy." *So much.*

❧

The sun was just beginning to set when Matt returned to Roswell. He'd had a lot of time to think on the ride home, and he became more frustrated with each mile he traveled. Emma was one of the most intelligent women he knew. Surely she'd thought of the risks involved in putting that advertisement in the paper. At the same time, he was angry with himself.

Emma was fully capable of keeping the promise she'd made to Annie, and he knew it. He needed to talk her out of this ridiculous mail-order scheme.

After cleaning up in his room at the boardinghouse, Matt checked in with Sheriff Haynes. He considered talking to him about Emma's advertisement but decided to wait until after he spoke with her.

Matt walked to Emma's café with long, purposeful strides. How many replies had she received to her advertisement? Did any of them sound promising? Had she already answered some?

The café was crowded when he entered, and he realized he'd have to wait to confront Emma. That wouldn't be difficult, he decided as his stomach rumbled in response to the appetizing smells that surrounded him.

He sat at his regular table just as Emma swung out of the kitchen, her arms loaded with plates from wrist to elbow. She delivered the orders to the table behind him. When she turned around, she stopped and stared at him.

Matt wasn't prepared for the tightness in his chest at the sight of her. His breath caught in his throat, and his heart started hammering. She seemed to be almost as glad to see him as he was to see her.

"Welcome back," she said as she wiped his table. "How'd it go?"

"Interesting," he said, thinking mostly about the copy of her advertisement in his shirt pocket. "How's Mandy?"

"She's wonderful. Growing every day." Emma rubbed her hands on her apron. "How was your trip?"

"Long. But everything went well." Matt noticed Emma was looking everywhere but at him and wondered why she was so distracted. "And how have things been with you? No problems?"

"None. Are you hungry? Or did you just stop by for coffee?"

I stopped by to tell you how crazy you are. But he couldn't say that. Not yet. He'd wait until he could talk to her alone. "I'd like some of whatever smells so good."

Emma grinned. "That's my new special, chicken and dumplings. It's been going over quite well."

"I'll have that. And a piece of pie, too, if you have any left."

"You're in luck. Liddy brought in an extra apple pie today." She darted off to the kitchen.

❧

"You all right, Miss Emma?" Ben asked as he ladled the chicken and dumplings onto a plate and added a hot biscuit. "You look a bit flushed."

"I'm fine." Emma did feel flushed. She tried to blame it on the heat in the kitchen and rushing around, but in truth, she knew it was from seeing Matt. She was glad he was back, but she wasn't happy that her pulse still raced at the sight of him. Would she ever get beyond that?

Well, she'd have to. If she was ever going to have a life with another man, she would have to stop pining over Deputy Matt Johnson.

She took the plate from Ben and headed back to the dining room. Matt was reading a torn piece of paper, but he quickly stuffed it into his shirt pocket as she approached with his meal.

"Here you go." Emma set the plate down. "I forgot to ask what you wanted to drink."

"Coffee would be nice."

Emma filled his cup, then took the pot around to her other customers. She kept as busy as she could and tried not to think of how right it seemed to have him taking supper at her café again.

When Matt was nearly through with his meal, Emma brought fresh coffee along with his pie.

"You could give lessons to the cook at the dining room I visited in Lincoln," he said. "The sign outside the hotel states they serve the best food in Lincoln County. If that's true, I'm glad I live here in Chaves County."

"Why, thank you, Matt. Ben is certainly an excellent cook. I'm surprised he hasn't opened his own restaurant by now."

She was called away by one of her other customers, then spent several minutes with people paying their bills. By the time everyone had cleared out, Matt was finishing up his pie. Emma flipped the CLOSED sign around to face the street.

She shook the coffeepot. "There's one more cup left. Would you like it?"

"No, I'm fine. Why don't you pour it for yourself and join me? There's something I need to talk to you about."

Emma wondered what Matt could possibly "need" to talk to her about. She poured herself the last of the coffee and sat across from him. When Matt pulled out the piece of paper he'd been looking at earlier, her heart slammed to a stop.

He slid the paper across the table so she could get a good look at it. Sure enough, it was a copy of her advertisement. When Emma's heart began to beat again, she held her breath, waiting for Matt to speak.

His voice was low and steely. "Have you lost your mind, Emma?"

Probably.

"Do you have any idea what kind of man might answer this?"

I've been mulling that over.

"What made you do something so crazy?"

Finally, Emma found her voice. "I will not let Douglas Harper take Mandy away from me. He said if I had a husband there would be no problem. Well, I'm going to find one."

"This way? Emma, you haven't thought this through—"

"What other way would you suggest?"

"You could have your pick of men in this town, Emma. You must know that."

Oh? How about you, Deputy? You've been my pick for years. Emma shook her head. "Do you see anyone beating down my door to propose? Besides, even if someone were inclined to offer marriage, Harper would probably pay him to get out of town."

"How long did you request for these ads to run?"

That's none of your business, she wanted to say. "One month."

Matt groaned. "And how many responses have you received so far?"

Emma wasn't about to tell him there'd been only one. "Does it matter?"

"You could wire the newspapers and have them pull the advertisement," he suggested.

Emma straightened her shoulders and lifted her chin. "I could. But I won't."

Matt took a deep breath. "All right. But if you insist on going through with this, at least let me or the sheriff check out the responses and see if any of these men are wanted for any crimes."

Emma prayed for calmness. How dare he interfere in her personal life. Why should she let him have a say in who she picked for a husband? She could choose someone by herself quite well, thank you very much!

Besides, there was nothing to check out at present, since she'd already decided not to reply to the one response she'd received. But she wasn't about to tell Deputy Matthew Johnson that.

"The whole point in putting in the advertisement was so I could do the choosing. I assure you I will not answer any responses that sound suspicious." Emma chewed her bottom lip. "There is something you could do for me, however."

Matt reached across the table and touched her hand. "Anything. What is it?"

"I decided not to put the advertisement in the Roswell papers, so I would appreciate it if you would keep this to yourself."

He leaned back in his chair and snorted. "I won't be talking to anyone about this—other than the sheriff."

"There's no need for him to know."

"Emma, you gave your name and city of residence in that advertisement. It wouldn't be hard for someone to come here and check *you* out."

Emma's heart sank to her stomach. Why hadn't she realized that? Well, that was one more detail she needed God to help her with.

"Just let us check out—"

"I appreciate your concern, Deputy, but I'm ready to close up now." Emma stood and picked up the pie plate and fork.

Matt stuffed the clipping back into his pocket and crammed his hat on his head. He tossed some coins onto the table to pay for his meal and marched toward the door. "I am going to talk to the sheriff about this, Emma. Maybe he can reason with you."

Emma locked the door behind him. She'd never seen Matt so angry, at least not at her. Well, she wasn't very happy with him, either.

❧

Matt stomped across the street to the office. Sheriff Haynes glanced up as he entered.

"You have to talk some sense into that woman," Matt said as he plunked down into the chair beside the desk.

"Oh?" The sheriff grinned. "And what woman is that?"

Matt handed him the advertisement.

Sheriff Haynes scanned the paper with a crinkled brow. "Why would Emma Hanson need to advertise for a husband? And why would she put her name right out there like that? Most of the men who place these kinds of ads just use their initials."

Matt pushed his hat back and rubbed his eyes. "She was in a panic over this town council thing. She's determined to keep Mandy, and she seems to think this is her answer."

The sheriff rocked back and forth in his chair, his brow smoothing. "Maybe it is."

"Marrying a complete stranger?" Matt shouted.

The sheriff chuckled. "You're worried about her, aren't you, Son?"

"Of course I am. I'd be worried about any woman who did such a fool thing." Just not quite as concerned as he was about Emma, Matt admitted to himself.

"We could check up on those who respond."

"I already suggested that to her. But she doesn't want to hear anything I have to say on the subject."

Sheriff Haynes snickered. "I'll have a talk with her tomorrow."

"Thanks." Matt took a gulp of coffee. It tasted horrible, as usual. "I think I'm going to go home and get some rest."

"Good idea."

Matt turned back at the door. "Oh, and she seems to think that because she didn't put it in the Roswell papers, no one here will find out about it."

The sheriff nodded. "Well, the news won't come from me."

❧

It didn't surprise Emma when Sheriff Haynes knocked on the kitchen door first thing the next morning, even before Ben arrived.

He tipped his hat. "Mornin', Miss Hanson. I was hoping to have a word with you before you opened up." He inhaled deeply. "That coffee sure smells good."

"Have a seat, Sheriff." She poured him a cup. "What can I do for you?"

"Well, with all due respect, I hope there's something I can do for you."

"Matt told you about the advertisement, didn't he?" Emma took a sip from her own up.

"He's right, you know. If you get any responses to that advertisement, you should let us check them out for you."

"Sheriff, did you offer to check out the advertisement Beth Morgan answered?"

"This is different."

"How so?"

The sheriff took a long drink of his coffee. "Beth chose to answer one person, and she might or might not regret it later. Maybe she should have come to us to check out that man first. But, Emma, by putting an advertisement in the paper yourself, you seem to be asking for trouble."

Emma motioned to the fenced-off area where Mandy was playing. "I'm determined to keep that child, Sheriff. And having a husband will make that possible."

"But, Emma, you want the best man to help raise her, don't you?"

"Of course I do. And I'm trusting that the Lord will send the right one."

"I believe God can do that. My problem is that you may think the wrong one is the right one. My job is to protect you. So just let me check out the letters before you read them. Men can be quite deceptive, and the Lord wouldn't want you to be misled."

Emma didn't want to tell him she'd destroyed the only response she'd received so far. But if other letters came in, she didn't want the sheriff, or his deputies, to inspect them before she had a chance to read them.

She watched Mandy playing with a rag doll Liddy had made her. *Lord, please help me know how to handle this.*

"So far there haven't been any letters I would consider answering," she said.

The sheriff drank his coffee in silence.

Certain she would never hear the end of it if she didn't agree, Emma finally said, "But if any interesting ones come in, I promise I'll show them to you."

Sheriff Haynes raised his cup. "Fair enough. And if you get any peculiar ones, you might think about bringing those over, too."

"I'll think about it."

He drained his cup and stood. "I trust you'll make the right decision. Deputy Johnson is certainly going to be relieved."

She saw the sheriff out, confident that she was doing the right thing. But she didn't like the idea that Matt might be gloating over her change of mind.

nine

"Mornin', Miss Emma," Ben said as he entered the kitchen. "Saw the sheriff leavin'. There ain't been no problem, has they?"

"No, Ben," Emma assured him, still mulling over her acquiescence to the sheriff's offer. "Everything's fine."

"That's good." He put the biscuits Emma had just cut into the oven. Then he started slicing bacon.

Emma took Mandy to the front and unlocked the door. She tickled the child on the way there and laughed at her giggles. No matter how gray the day seemed, all she had to do was cuddle Mandy close and the day suddenly brightened. How she loved this child!

She kept Mandy with her while she took her first few orders, but when business began to pick up, she settled the little girl in the kitchen with her toys. Hallie and Ben always gave her plenty of attention while they worked in the kitchen. No one could say Mandy wasn't well taken care of, even when she didn't have Emma's complete attention.

❧

Matt entered the sheriff's office yawning.

"Morning, Deputy," Sheriff Haynes greeted him. "You don't look like you slept very well last night."

Matt took off his hat. "Kept worrying about that headstrong woman across the street."

"Well, I had a talk with her this morning."

Matt's heart jumped. "Did she agree to bring all the letters to us?"

Sheriff Haynes drummed his fingers on the desk. "Not exactly."

Matt slapped his hat against his thigh. "Stubborn woman," he muttered.

"Now, hold on. No need to get riled up. She did agree to let us check the ones she might respond to."

"That's something, I guess." Matt knew he should feel better. But he didn't. "Did she give you any of the letters?"

"No. Said there hadn't been any she wanted to reply to."

Matt released the breath he'd been holding.

"I've been thinking, though," the sheriff said. "With her name and the town in the advertisement, anyone could come check her out."

Matt's stomach started to burn. That thought had kept him awake half the night—until he'd found himself praying about it. After he asked God to watch over Emma, he'd finally drifted off to sleep.

"I think maybe we'd better keep a closer eye on her place," the sheriff said.

"Good idea," Matt agreed.

"Shouldn't be too hard." Sheriff Haynes grinned. "She has the best food in town. Now I know why you spend so much time over there."

That's what I've always told myself. Deep down, Matt knew there was much more than good food that kept him going back to Emma's café. He'd been fighting his attraction to her for years. He just couldn't let himself act on his feelings.

But now she was determined to find a husband. And he was going to have to accept that fact, whether he liked it or not. At least he could try to make certain she didn't pick the wrong kind of man. Trouble was, he wasn't sure there would be a right kind for her. To his way of thinking, no man was good enough for Emma Hanson.

Matt noticed the sheriff smirking at him. What had they been discussing? Oh, yes. Food. "After tasting 'the best food in Lincoln,' it was nice to get back to Emma's café. I won't mind checking in a little more often."

Sheriff Haynes smiled. "I didn't think you would. It's just too bad the town council is being so narrow-minded about Annie's child."

"You know, we've both had a firsthand look at how well Emma's taking care of Mandy. At the next council meeting, we could assure the council members of how well they're both doing."

"We could do that. But I wouldn't count on it changing minds. Part of the problem is what they consider the baby's 'questionable background.' Just between you and me, I think some of those men might be wondering if they could be that child's father. They'd want to get her out of town before she grows up to look like them."

Matt had never thought of that.

"Truth is, Mandy looks just like her mama," Sheriff Haynes continued.

"Even if she did grow up to resemble someone, there's no way of knowing for sure who the father was. Can't they see that?"

"Fear doesn't reason, Matt. That's why we need to keep a watchful eye on Emma. She could be in as much danger from a councilman as she might be from an unknown suitor."

"I could use some breakfast. Mind if I take the first watch?"

"Go ahead. I'll go over at noontime."

❧

Emma saw Matt crossing the street toward her café. Was he coming to gloat because she'd agreed to let the sheriff do some checking?

He took off his hat when he entered the café. Since his usual table was taken, he chose a seat near the kitchen. "Good morning, Emma. Could I get some flapjacks and bacon, please?"

"Coming right up." Emma poured Matt's coffee, then left to give Ben the order.

When his food was ready, she brought it out with a tub of butter and a small pitcher of syrup. Setting it all down in front of him, she steeled herself for any remarks he might make.

"Thank you." He began to spread butter on his pancakes. Apparently, he wasn't going to rub it in.

Emma busied herself with filling the other customers' cups of coffee.

Matt finished his meal and paid for it. "Have a good day, Emma."

"You too, Deputy." She breathed a sigh of relief when he walked out the door without saying a word about the advertisement.

The rest of the day went smoothly. At midmorning, when Liddy brought in her sweets, she coaxed Emma into taking a break. Since business had thinned out, Emma brought Mandy out and held her while she enjoyed a cup of tea with her friend.

"Oh, Em, she's growing so fast," Liddy said, watching the baby bounce on Emma's lap.

"She's going to be walking any day now. She pulls herself

around the play area already."

Mandy bobbed her head and chortled as if she knew exactly what Emma was saying. Liddy's two-year-old son reached out and touched Mandy's foot.

"Your baby is growing up, too," Emma said.

"He certainly is." Liddy watched her toddler playing with Mandy's foot. Mandy giggled at the little boy's attention, and he laughed along with her.

"Oh, Liddy, wouldn't it be wonderful if they married each other when they grew up?"

Liddy gazed at the two children. "It'd be a blessing for us, that's for sure. Speaking of marriage, have you received any responses to your advertisement yet?"

"Just one. I tore it up." As Emma told about the letter, Liddy pursed her lips, obviously trying hard not to chuckle.

"Go ahead and laugh. It's what I deserve for doing such a silly thing."

"I'm sorry, Em. I'm sure you're going to get some wonderful answers soon."

Emma rubbed her temple. "Matt found my advertisement in a paper in Lincoln. He told the sheriff about it, and he came to see me. I promised to let him check out any letters I might consider answering. Assuming I get any more."

"That's a good idea." Liddy took a sip of tea. "What was Matt's reaction to the advertisement?"

"He seemed angry."

"That's interesting."

"Liddy, don't read anything into it. There's nothing there." Emma changed the subject. "How are Amy and Grace doing?"

"Really well. They're such good girls. They'll be a lot of help with the new—" Liddy clapped her hand over her mouth.

"Liddy? Are you expecting?"

She lowered her hand and whispered, "I haven't even told Cal. Don't tell a soul, promise?"

"Of course I won't. Oh, Liddy, I'm so happy for you!" Cal and Liddy had proven how much they could love each other's children, and Emma was thrilled they would now have one of their own to add to the mix.

"I guess I'd better plan a really nice meal tonight, so I can tell him and the children before I blurt it out to anyone else." She grinned at her little boy. "Come on, Son, let's find your daddy so I can get home and start cooking."

After Liddy left, Emma asked Ben to watch the front so she could check her mail. Not bothering with the carriage, she carried Mandy the few blocks to the post office.

Her heart skittered when she was handed four letters. She'd wait until evening to read them. Who knew? Maybe one of these was from the man the Lord was sending into her and Mandy's life.

‿

Sitting on the porch outside the sheriff's office, Matt watched Emma come out of the post office and cross the street with Mandy in her arms. She held envelopes in her hand. Were they answers to her advertisement? His chest tightened. He crossed the street and headed down the boardwalk toward her.

He tipped his hat. "Looks like you got some mail today."

Mandy grinned at him and giggled. She was an adorable baby; no doubt about it.

"A little."

That was it. Nothing more. He tipped his hat again. "Guess I'd better get back to work." He tweaked the little girl's nose. "Good-bye, Miss Mandy."

"Bye-bye." Mandy waved at him.

"See you for dinner, Emma." Matt crossed the street once more. If she'd received answers to her advertisement, Emma wasn't telling. He'd just have to wait and see if any of them were interesting enough to check out.

&

The rest of the day, Emma's spirits were high, and she often found herself patting the letters in her pocket. She would read them that night and see if any were promising enough to answer. She had to keep her thoughts on those letters. Otherwise, they kept returning to the deputy who sat across the room eating his supper.

She knew he was curious about the letters, and she had expected him to ask if they were replies to her advertisement. But to Matt's credit, he hadn't mentioned them. And she hadn't volunteered any information.

As she was bustling around trying to get everyone waited on, she heard a loud cry from the kitchen. She and Matt got there at the same time. Hallie was holding a crying Mandy.

"I don't know what's wrong, Miss Emma. I was feeding her supper and she just puckered up and started crying."

"She did that earlier today, too." When Emma took Mandy, the baby's cries eased up for a moment. But when she tried to give the baby a spoonful of food, she started crying again. Emma stuck a finger in her mouth, being careful to miss the four front teeth. Before she could check out her back gums, Mandy jerked her head away and cried harder. "I think she may be cutting a new tooth." Emma wondered if Annie had gone through this same fussiness with Mandy when her first four teeth came in.

When Mandy saw Matt, she stopped crying, hiccupped,

and reached out to him.

Matt appeared a little flustered as he took her, but he grinned broadly when she buried her head in his shoulder.

"Well, I'll be." Ben chuckled.

"I'll take her, Matt," Emma said, reaching for the baby. "You need to get back to work." But Mandy turned away from Emma and switched to Matt's other shoulder.

Matt's smile broadened. "I'm fine. Let me hold her awhile. I don't mind. Really."

Hallie reached into the icebox and chipped off a piece of ice. She wrapped it in a clean cloth and gave it to Matt. "See if she'll suck on this. It might ease her some."

Emma wasn't sure what to do. She wanted to be the one to comfort Mandy, but at that moment the little girl seemed to want Matt. As soon as the last few customers left, she would start closing up. On second thought, she could put the CLOSED sign out now. After all, it was her business. If her child needed her, she'd just lock the door.

Matt, Hallie, and Ben seemed to have things under control in the kitchen. "I'll close up as soon as those last two people leave."

Matt took a seat at the kitchen table and patted Mandy on the back. "She'll be fine, Emma. Go take care of your customers."

Mandy closed her eyes and smiled. Emma slipped out to the front. If she didn't know better, she'd think that child had staged the whole crying bit just to get into Matt's arms. She chuckled to herself. Maybe she should take some lessons from the baby.

She flipped the OPEN sign around and locked the door. She would let her last customers out when they were ready, but she wanted to make sure she didn't get any others. Before she could ask if they needed anything else, the Harrisons approached the counter, ready to pay.

"Is the baby all right?" Nelda asked.

"She's fine. Just teething. But I'm closing up early so I can try to ease her gums."

"It's time we were headed home anyway," Jim said, taking his change.

Emma saw them out, then locked the door and returned to the kitchen.

Mandy was fast asleep in Matt's arms. With his eyes closed, he rocked her back and forth. Ben and Hallie were quietly cleaning up the kitchen, with Hallie humming softly. Emma stopped in the doorway and soaked up the peacefulness of the scene. She hated to disturb it.

She touched Matt's shoulder gently. "It's all right," she whispered. "I can take her now."

His eyelids flew open and he cleared his throat. "She's fine for the moment. Do you want me to carry her upstairs?"

"It might be easier that way, Miss Emma," Hallie said. "She sure seems to be resting good."

Emma shrugged. "All right. Follow me. I'll get her bed ready."

She climbed the stairs ahead of Matt and turned down Mandy's covers. After he lowered Mandy into the crib, Emma covered her and bent to kiss her forehead.

She was almost surprised when she turned around and found Matt waiting for her. She'd expected him to hightail it downstairs, as he'd done the last time. Leaving the door to the apartment open so she could hear if Mandy cried out, she went back down the stairs, Matt close behind her.

As they reached the bottom step, Emma said, "Thank you, Matt."

"You're welcome. She's a sweetheart, isn't she?"

"I think so. Would you like a cup of coffee before you go?"

"No, thank you. I've been having trouble sleeping lately. I think I'll pass."

Matt told Ben and Hallie good night, then headed for the back door. Emma followed.

"See you tomorrow," he said. "I hope Mandy sleeps well."

"So do I. Thank you again."

"It was my pleasure. I've never put a baby to sleep before." He settled his hat on his head and tipped the brim to her. "Good night."

Ben and Hallie took off for home, and Emma headed back upstairs. She readied herself for bed, then opened the pack of letters and started reading. After a few minutes, she set them on her bedside table. It was hard to concentrate on what any of them said when her thoughts kept going back over the evening.

Emma couldn't get the picture of Matt holding Mandy out of her mind. Somehow she knew it would be with her for a very long time.

ten

Mandy slept fitfully that night. First thing the next morning, Emma placed a call to Doc Bradshaw. She was sure Mandy was probably just teething but wanted to make certain. He told her to come right over.

Emma left the café in Ben's care. The morning air felt cool; fall was coming soon. She'd have to buy warmer clothes for Mandy before long.

"Oh, my, how she's growing," Myrtle exclaimed as she let Emma in. "You're doing an excellent job."

"Thank you. She's a precious baby. But she hasn't been feeling well lately, so I wanted to have Doc check her out."

"There's just one patient ahead of you. He should be finished shortly." Myrtle reached out to Mandy. "Do you think she'll let me hold her?"

Mandy answered by reaching out her hands to the woman.

"How sweet she is." Myrtle hugged her close.

Emma watched Mandy play with Myrtle's collar. "She's a wonderful baby. I'm honored that Annie trusted me to raise her."

Myrtle lowered her voice as if there were someone else in the room to overhear. "You did see the notice in the paper that there's another council meeting called for this Monday, didn't you?"

"No. I haven't had time to read the paper much lately. Surely they wouldn't hold a meeting about Mandy's future without officially notifying me." Emma's heart started beating hard.

"I don't know. But I wouldn't put it past Harper." Myrtle bustled into the parlor to get the newspaper and showed Emma the article. "If I hear anything about a change of agenda, I'll let you know."

"Thank you."

Mandy started fussing and reached for Emma. Emma took the child and jiggled her in her arms. "It's all right, Baby. Doc will see you soon."

"I'll do that right now," Doc said as he came out of his office with his other patient. "Take her on into my office, Emma. I'll be right with you."

Emma had barely sat down before Doc came in. "Now, what seems to be the problem with this young'un?"

"I think she's cutting some teeth, but I'm new at this, so I wanted to check with you to make sure it's not something else."

"Well, let's find out."

Emma held Mandy while Doc checked her over. When he was finished, he confirmed that she was indeed teething, but otherwise she was fit as a fiddle. "She's flourishing in your care, Emma. Annie would be very pleased."

Tears sprang to Emma's eyes. "Thank you. That means a lot to me."

Doc Bradshaw cleared his throat. "You can try using a little vanilla extract on those gums." He went to his medicine cabinet and handed her a small vial. "If that doesn't ease her, try this. It's called paregoric. Put a tiny drop of it on a clean rag and try to rub it on her gums. It should ease her until the teeth cut all the way through. Don't be surprised if she sleeps a little more than usual."

"Thank you, Doc. What do I owe you?"

"Oh, I'll bring Myrtle over to the café for a meal one of these days; how's that?"

"That would be fine," Emma said, bundling Mandy back up. "I'll be expecting you."

She started back to the café, relieved that Mandy was all right except for the painful teething she was going through. Her thoughts were so focused on the baby, she didn't see Harper crossing the street until she almost bumped into him.

"Miss Hanson, I see you've come from the doctor. Is anything wrong with the child?"

Emma was sure he would latch on to any reason at all to think she wasn't taking care of Mandy. "She's doing beautifully. She's teething, and Doc gave me something to make her more comfortable."

"Oh? I'm sure that isn't pleasant." Harper reached out to cup Mandy's cheek with his hand. She must have thought he was handing her something to chew on because she turned and chomped down on his thumb.

"Ouch!" Harper howled. "You little minx."

Mandy started crying. Emma gathered her closer. "I told you she was teething, Mr. Harper. Now you've made her cry. If you'll excuse us, I need to get some medicine on her gums."

Emma rushed along the boardwalk, relieved to get away from the man. When she reached the café door, she looked back to see Harper, his meaty thumb in his mouth, marching toward Doc's place. Emma admonished herself for not feeling bad for the man. Hard as she tried, she couldn't work up any sympathy for him.

૨૦

Matt walked out of the sheriff's office and looked down the

street. He saw Emma run into Harper. The revulsion he felt at seeing the man standing so close to Emma and the baby made him start barreling down the boardwalk.

When he saw Harper touch the baby, a desire to protect Mandy and Emma hit him with such force he almost started running. But when Harper howled, it was quickly apparent who had the upper hand. Matt tried to contain the laughter that fought to burst forth as he realized Mandy had bit the man. When he saw the ugly expression on Harper's face as he yelled at Emma and Mandy, the urge to laugh changed quickly to an itch to grab that menace by the neck.

Matt lengthened his stride, but Emma seemed to have everything under control before he was halfway to them. She took off down the other side of the street as Harper headed in the opposite direction.

Emma was quite a woman. And it looked like Mandy was going to hold her own in this world, too. Matt chuckled as he entered the café for breakfast.

He caught the smell of vanilla when he peeked into the kitchen. Emma was trying to apply something on a cloth to Mandy's mouth. The baby smiled when she saw Matt standing in the doorway, which enabled Emma to get the cloth back to where it needed to be.

"There! That should make you feel better soon."

"Shouldn't you put some kind of disinfectant on her, too?" Matt tweaked Mandy on the nose.

"I beg your pardon?" Emma put the top back on the bottle of vanilla.

"Well, you never know what germs biting Harper might have exposed her to."

The corners of her mouth curled upward. "You saw that?"

Matt nodded. "And heard the yowl."

"Oh, wasn't that priceless?" Emma chuckled. Her laughter ignited Matt's, and soon they were holding their sides, with Mandy giggling right along with them, as if she knew what was so funny. Emma brought Ben and Hallie up-to-date between gasps.

When the door to the dining room opened and Beth Morgan peeked around it, they tried to get their laughter under control.

"Miss Emma?" Beth said hesitantly. "You have several customers out here. Would you like me to take their orders?"

"Oh, that's sweet of you, Beth." Emma handed Mandy to Hallie. "But no need; I'll be right there."

Matt slapped Ben on the shoulder. "I'll save Emma from having to take my order. How about some pancakes and bacon for me, Ben?"

"Comin' right up, Deputy." Ben began stirring the bowl of batter on the counter by the stove.

A few more giggles managed to escape as Matt followed Emma out the door and took a seat at his usual table. "That's some child you've got there."

"She's very intuitive, isn't she?" Emma grinned, then went to check on her other customers.

Matt ate his breakfast, snickering every so often as he watched Emma go about her business.

☙

Emma chuckled off and on all day, every time she remembered the look on Harper's face when Mandy took a chunk out of his thumb. She hoped the child didn't get sick. He'd probably make an issue about it at the meeting on Monday.

The vanilla made Mandy smell wonderful, but the poor little thing was still fussy, so Emma decided to use the paregoric and put her down for a nap.

It wasn't until the afternoon lull that Emma remembered her letters. She ran upstairs to get them. On the way she stopped to check on Mandy. The medicine seemed to have worked, as she was sleeping soundly, like Doc said she would.

Emma sat at a table in the dining room with a cup of tea and started reading the letters. Two of the respondents asked if she would be willing to relocate her business, and one wanted to know what kind of business she owned. The last one sounded sweet and sincere, but the sender wanted her to move to a ranch near Eddy to help him raise his five children. None of the letters struck a chord in her.

The sheriff came in just as she finished reading the letters. He sat across from her. "Anything there we need to check into for you?"

Emma shook her head. "There's one I'll reply to, but only because it seems the right thing to do. I won't be asking him to answer."

"Either way, it'd be best if you'd let us check our wanted files."

Why not let the sheriff's office do a check, even if it was on someone she didn't intend to continue a correspondence with? She picked up the letter she'd like best and slipped it out of the envelope, then handed the envelope to the sheriff. She tucked the letter, along with the other three, back into her apron pocket. "All right."

He studied the return address. "I'll get it back to you as soon as I can."

"That's fine." There was no rush as far as she was concerned, but Emma didn't tell the sheriff that. She left him to his coffee and went upstairs to check on Mandy.

The baby was still sleeping peacefully, and Emma was relieved that her pain had eased enough for her to sleep soundly. Leaving Ben and Hallie in charge, she slipped out the back door to make a quick trip to the post office. She was pleased to find four more responses waiting for her.

She entered the café and shuffled through the envelopes. There were two from the Lincoln area, one from Eddy, and one from Hondo. She stuck them in her skirt pocket and headed for the kitchen.

During the evening lull, she pulled the letters out of her pocket and tore open one of the envelopes. It was from a rancher near Hondo. He couldn't leave his ranch, but maybe she could get someone to run her business and join him. *"It sure is lonely out here."*

She'd felt lonely, too, before she started taking care of Mandy. But Emma didn't want to leave Roswell.

The next letter was from a man in Eddy. He ran a livery stable and wondered if Emma might want to merge her business into his. His stilted wording gave her the impression he wanted a career partner more than a wife.

One of the men from Lincoln asked all kinds of questions. Was she a good cook? How many children did she have? What kind of business did she run, and how many people would it support? She had to give him credit. He wanted to understand what he might be getting into, same as she did.

Emma blew the bangs off her forehead. None of the letters appealed to her enough to answer. But she'd keep them, just in case. They might be the best of the lot—or the last.

&

Matt knew Emma didn't see him walk in. She was too interested in the mail she was reading. She held several letters, and one seemed to interest her more than the others.

"Emma?"

She glanced up at him and then back down at the letter, folding it and sliding it back into its envelope. A delicate color spread across her cheekbones. "What can I get you, Deputy?"

"Whatever Ben has ready will be fine." He took a seat across from her and reached into his shirt pocket, pulling out the envelope the sheriff had asked him to bring back to her. "Sheriff Haynes said to tell you this one is all clear."

Emma took the envelope and added it to her stack. She slipped all of the letters into her apron pocket. "Thank you."

"He also said you should let us know when you need anyone else checked out."

"I'll do that."

Matt watched her go to the kitchen, wishing he knew what was in the letters she seemed to be guarding so closely. Had someone captured her interest?

The bell above the door jingled, and he looked up to see Douglas Harper enter, his thumb thickly wrapped in gauze. Anger welled up in Matt. If it weren't for Harper, Emma wouldn't have put that advertisement in the paper.

The councilman headed straight for the kitchen, but Matt stood to halt his progress. "Anything I can help you with?"

"I need to talk to Miss Hanson." He took another step toward the kitchen.

Matt stopped him again. "She'll be right out. She's bringing me dinner."

Harper kept walking. Matt moved to block the kitchen door just as Emma flung it open. She bumped into Matt and he lost his footing for a moment, knocking him into Harper. The banker held up his bandaged hand to ward Matt off. It didn't work. As Matt righted himself, his shoulder caught Harper's thumb and bent it back. Harper yelped in pain, then uttered a string of expletives.

"Mr. Harper!" Matt cried. "I realize you're hurting, but you need to apologize to Miss Hanson for using foul language in her presence and in her establishment."

"Apologize? To her? I got this injury because that brat she's raising bit me! She's the one who owes me an apology."

Emma set down the tray she'd managed not to drop. "I apologize for Mandy biting you, Mr. Harper. But I can assure you it wasn't intentional on her part. You did put your thumb in close proximity to her mouth, and teething babies like to chew."

Matt put his hand on the councilman's shoulder, desperate to get him out of Emma's café. "Come on, Harper. I'll walk you over to Doc's, and we'll have him check out that thumb."

Harper jerked away from Matt. "I've already seen Dr. Bradshaw about this injury." He pulled a piece of paper out of his pants pocket. "As a matter of fact, I came over to give Emma this bill. Since the child in her care bit me, it only seems fitting that she pay for my treatment. However, since I have to have my injury rechecked now, I will bring the total bill by later." He tossed the receipt on the counter, then lumbered out the door, holding his bandaged thumb.

"Why, that beats all." Matt shook his head. "He expects you to pay for him practically inviting Mandy to bite him?"

"Don't worry about it." Emma took his plate off the tray and set it on his table. "Eat your dinner while it's still hot."

"But—"

"It's all right. Mandy is my responsibility, and she did bite him. I'll pay Doc." She freshened the coffee in his half-empty cup. "Besides, the expression on his face will be worth every penny."

Matt chuckled. "You're right. In that case, I'll help pay the bill."

Emma's smile faded. "I don't think this will help my cause, though. Harper is going to be more determined than ever to take Mandy away."

She reached into her apron pocket and pulled out the letters. She slid each one out of its envelope and handed all the envelopes to Matt, except the one he'd brought back to her. "Could you have the sheriff check these out, please?"

Matt's heart seemed to dive into his stomach. This was what he'd wanted, wasn't it? To be able to check out the men who answered her advertisement? Actually, he'd been hoping no one would respond. Even though he knew some would, he wasn't the least bit happy about it. He took the envelopes. "Certainly."

Emma left him to wait on a couple of late customers. Matt peered down at his plate. Everything smelled delicious. But for some reason, his appetite had disappeared.

eleven

Matt's appetite didn't improve much over the next few days. The stack of letters Emma brought back from the post office seemed to grow with each passing day, as did the number of envelopes she sent over to be checked out.

His stomach churned when he came in for an afternoon break and found her at a table writing a letter. She seemed distracted as she got up to serve him a piece of chocolate cake and a cup of coffee. When she went back to her letter writing after barely acknowledging him, Matt was sure she'd decided to reply to one of the men who'd answered her advertisement. He fought the jealousy he could no longer deny.

He kept telling himself he should be happy for her. Finding a husband would get the council off her back, and she wouldn't be raising Mandy alone. That had been his main concern, hadn't it? That raising the baby by herself would be too hard on Emma?

But that was before he'd watched her and seen that she could handle the challenge.

The thought of Emma marrying anyone who wasn't good enough for her or Mandy, who didn't realize how special they both were, had Matt's stomach burning and his temper on edge. He was almost as mad at himself as he was at the council. He should have stood up for her. He knew Emma's character. There'd been no doubt that she would do everything in her power to keep the promise she'd made to Annie.

The next council meeting was only a few days away. He'd be there, and this time he wasn't leaving in the middle. He couldn't let them take Mandy away from Emma or force her into marrying someone she didn't even know.

Until then, he'd make sure Harper didn't cause her any more problems. And he'd try to get his frustration under control.

He forced down a bite of pie, his stomach rumbling. Maybe he should see if Doc had anything to cure his awful heartache—that is, *heartburn.*

૨઼

Emma's heart sank. None of these letters lit even a tiny spark of interest. Oh, some were nice, and she was sure the men who wrote them were, too. But there was nothing in the letters that made her want to answer them. Still, she needed to find one or two, at least to see if a correspondence might spur some interest that a single letter wouldn't. The council meeting was coming up soon. If she answered at least one letter, she could honestly say she was trying to find someone suitable.

Trouble was, the right person was sitting across the room, staring out the window with a frown on his face. Matt was so wonderful with Mandy, always asking how she was feeling, wanting to look in on her. He'd even fed her a few times over the last few days. He seemed to especially like it when she fell asleep in his arms.

Emma couldn't deny that her feelings were deepening for the lanky deputy, even though she knew they'd never be reciprocated. She pulled a piece of paper toward her. Dipping her pen in ink, she began to reply to the letter in front of her. Matt wasn't going to suddenly declare his undying love for her, and Harper wasn't going to let up on trying to take Mandy

away. She had no choice but to make an effort to find someone. Time was running out.

"Emma, could I bother you for a cup of tea?" Matt interrupted her train of thought.

"Tea?"

"Yes, please. My stomach isn't taking well to coffee this
afternoon."

"I'll be right out with it." Emma slipped the letter she'd
been writing into her apron pocket and hurried to the kitchen.
Ben was handing Mandy a wooden spoon and pan to play
with. The little girl loved banging and making a racket. Each
time she hit the pan, Ben held his hands over his ears.

"I peeked out, Miss Emma, and there weren't no customers,
'cept for the deputy. I figured he wouldn't mind a little noise."

"Not at all, Ben," Matt said from the doorway. "I did have
to come check out who was making all that commotion,
though."

Mandy grinned up at Matt and hit the pan extra hard. Emma
poured Matt a cup of tea and handed it to him. "I'm sorry your
stomach is feeling poorly. Maybe you ought to check with
Doc about it."

"I'll be fine," he answered in a husky voice. "It's good to
see her playing again. Did that tooth come through yet?"

"Yes," Emma replied. "I heard it clink against the spoon
when I fed her some oatmeal this morning."

Matt patted Mandy on the head. "I sure am glad that old
tooth decided to come through, Mandy baby."

The little girl stopped banging the pan and gazed up at Matt
adoringly. Emma's heart twisted. What would it be like to be
married to this man? To share her days and nights with him,
to have him help her raise Mandy?

Whoa. I can't let myself think that way. Matt had no intentions of marrying. Emma felt sorry for him. He might not realize it, but he needed someone to love him, someone to take care of him.

Matt glanced over his shoulder and raised an eyebrow at Emma. "Good thing Harper didn't pick today to put that thumb so close to Mandy's mouth."

Emma chuckled. "With five teeth instead of four, she might have just taken it clean off," she joked.

Matt drank a few sips of the tea, then handed the cup back to her. "I'd better get back to work."

Emma followed him to the front counter. "I hope you feel better soon."

He paid for his food, tipped his hat, and took his leave.

Emma watched him cross the street. Something about the way his shoulders slumped made her wonder if he was all right. Something certainly seemed to be bothering him. Perhaps he was lonely. Stubborn man. He needed someone as much as she and Mandy did. As she gazed out the window, she prayed the Lord would send the right person into Matt's life, to make him see he could keep his job and have love, too. At the moment it didn't even matter if it was her or someone else.

Emma sat at the kitchen table to finish her letter. She almost hoped she wouldn't get a reply, yet she prayed she'd get a letter from *someone* who would touch her heart and get her thoughts off the man who'd just left the café.

⁂

Doc assured Matt that he wasn't seriously ill but was probably just suffering from heartburn. He gave him some medicine and told him to cut down on his coffee intake.

"There's a substance in coffee called *caffeine,*" Doc explained, "that acts as a stimulant on the nervous system. When taken in small amounts, it's harmless for most people. In large amounts, however, it can cause nervousness and loss of sleep. It may also create headaches and digestive disturbances."

"I had no idea," Matt muttered. "Guess I'd better start drinking tea, huh?"

Doc smirked. "Tea contains a smaller percentage of caffeine than coffee, but it still has some. Your best bet is to start drinking milk."

Matt's eyes flew open. "Milk?"

Doc patted Matt's back. " 'Fraid so, Deputy."

Matt returned to the sheriff's office and took two of the pills Doc had given him, washing them down with a tall glass of water from the pump. He was sure it would alleviate the heartburn, but he didn't think anything could take away the heaviness in his heart. A lawman he was and a lawman he intended to stay, but he wasn't sure he could remain in Roswell and watch Emma make a life with some strange man. Yet he wasn't ready to consider leaving this place that had become home.

That afternoon Matt strolled to the end of Main Street, making his usual rounds. The saloons were quiet, not usually getting rowdy until evening.

The Gem served food in a dining room adjoining the bar. The cooking wasn't anything to brag about, and the clientele consisted mostly of saloon patrons who needed to sober up some before they went home. Usually, the place was quite busy. Customers from the Oasis Saloon, on the other side of the Gem, often came in for a bite to eat.

Matt sauntered into the dining area and was surprised to

find it occupied by several of the town council members. Douglas Harper sat at a round table in the middle of the room, talking with Homer Williams and Ed Bagley.

"Afternoon, gentlemen," Matt said with a tip of his Stetson. "I thought your meeting was scheduled for Monday night."

"It is," Homer Williams said. "We're just discussing a few things aforehand." If Homer's wife knew where he was, she'd be dragging him out by the ear. The same thing could be said about several of the men gathered there.

Matt took a seat at a table across the room. He ordered a bowl of stew, then picked up a newspaper someone had left there and pretended to read. He didn't want to appear to be eavesdropping, but as deputy sheriff, that's what he did a lot of the time.

He only heard bits and pieces of conversation, but he couldn't move closer without raising suspicion. He heard something about the stretch of railroad up in Amarillo that'd be finished in a little over a year, and something about prime property. Matt recalled Harper bragging that he'd bought up a fair amount of land in and around Roswell over the past few years. Rumor was, it hadn't always been what the owners wanted. Matt wondered what property he was talking about now.

Matt's stew arrived, and after staring at the layer of grease on top, he pushed the bowl to the side.

As he turned the page of the newspaper he was pretending to read, Jed Brewster entered the room. . .not from the saloon entrance but from the street. The other councilmen rose to leave, but Harper remained seated at the table. When Jed took one of the vacated chairs, Harper welcomed him as if he'd been expecting him.

Harper glanced in Matt's direction, and the deputy pulled his stew close and pretended to take a spoonful. The banker said something to Jed, too quiet for Matt to hear. The younger man shook his head in response.

Harper slid an envelope across the table to Jed, who pushed it back and stood. "You'll have to find someone else," Jed said with disgust. "I'm not interested." He stomped out the door.

"You'll be sorry," Harper called to Jed's back. When the door slammed behind him, Harper lowered his head and tried to discreetly tuck the envelope into his inside jacket pocket. Then he glanced around the room. When his eyes met Matt's, he scowled, rose, and exited the saloon.

Matt threw some coins onto the table to pay for the stew he hadn't eaten, then headed outside. Harper hadn't made it very far—he'd stopped a few yards down the street to talk to Zeke Anderson. Zeke owned a small farm just outside of town. It was rumored that he gambled away most of his earnings.

Harper handed Zeke an envelope similar to the one he'd tried to give to Jed, then ambled down the street.

A few strides farther, Harper handed another envelope to Robert Morris, an older gentleman who dabbled in real estate in the area.

Matt hurried back to the office and told Sheriff Haynes what he'd seen.

"Perhaps he was just handing out invitations to the council meeting," the sheriff suggested.

"I don't think so," Matt argued. "The meeting's open to all townspeople. No invitations are required."

The sheriff rubbed a hand over the stubble on his chin. "Harper's up to something. And it sounds like it might involve some more real estate ventures. Course, there's not much land left around Roswell he hasn't already tried to purchase. I guess he could be starting to buy up more property in town. Nothing wrong with that, but I don't trust the man's ethics. We'll have to keep an eye on him."

"Yes, sir." Matt rubbed his chin. He figured it wouldn't hurt to pay a little visit to Jed Brewster. He'd just have to be real subtle about it.

※

Emma was delighted to see Cal and Liddy and their children enter the café that evening. She took them to the best table and winked at Liddy. "Celebrating anything special tonight?"

"We sure are." Cal was beaming. "My wife is expecting."

"That's wonderful news!" Emma acted surprised as she hugged Cal and Liddy.

"Thanks," Liddy whispered into Emma's ear.

"You're in luck tonight. We have a couple of choices. Fried chicken or pork chops, with panfried potatoes, green beans, biscuits, and corn bread. My treat."

Cal pulled a chair out for his wife. "Emma, we can't let you—"

"Oh, yes, you can. After all the Sundays I've had supper with you?"

"Well, I guess it'd be all right, then." Liddy arched an eyebrow at her. "Providing you eat with us again this Sunday."

Emma knew better than to argue with Liddy when she raised that eyebrow. "Mandy and I will be happy to have dinner with you after church."

After Emma took their orders, Liddy added, "If Mandy isn't asleep, bring her out. Grace and Amy will entertain her. And bring a plate for yourself so you can join us. I'm sure

Hallie could wait on your other customers so you can have supper with us."

Emma brought out Mandy and her high chair. The baby loved Cal and Liddy's children and was quite happy with the extra attention. Emma headed back to the kitchen to help Ben dish up the plates. When she brought out the food, she found Matt sitting at the McAllisters' table next to Mandy's high chair.

"We asked Deputy Johnson to help us celebrate," Liddy said, barely holding back a grin.

Emma smiled at Matt as she distributed the meals. "Wonderful news, isn't it?"

"Sure is." He seemed to be feeling better than he had the last time he'd been in her café.

"What can I get for you?"

"I'll try the pork chops. . .and a glass of milk, please."

Maybe he wasn't feeling better. "Coming right up."

Emma fixed herself a plate and brought it out with Matt's, then sat on the other side of Mandy. Matt had already started feeding her some mashed-up fried potatoes.

Emma offered the little girl a piece of biscuit, but Mandy shook her curly little head. "No. Wan Matt."

Everyone at the table laughed. "Emma, I do believe that child of yours has a mind of her own," Liddy said.

"Just like her Em-mama," Matt said with a wink.

Emma swallowed around the lump in her throat. It almost felt as if she and Matt and Mandy were a family, like Liddy and Cal and their children. She knew it wasn't real, but how wonderful it felt to imagine it for just a moment.

"Have you received any good mail lately?" Liddy whispered.

Emma glanced at Matt, but he and Cal were carrying on

their own conversation, so she felt safe in answering. "Nothing really."

"Oh, Em, I'm sorry. But don't give up hope. I know the Lord is going to send the perfect man for you and Mandy. Just hang on."

"I'm trying, Liddy. With that council meeting on Monday night—"

"Don't you worry about that, either. Cal and I will be going with you, and there's no way we're going to let them take Mandy from you."

"But Harper seems so determined—"

"That nasty man had better not mess with us or the people we care about."

Emma was grateful for her friends, and she knew they would stand beside her. But she'd need more than their help if she were to keep Mandy. She needed the Lord to intervene.

"Are you pretty ladies talking about Douglas Harper?" Cal asked.

Liddy patted Emma's arm. "She's worried about the meeting on Monday."

"That man has been acting suspicious lately," Matt said.

"What's that scoundrel doing now?" Cal asked.

Matt rested his elbows on the table and leaned in. "I overheard him mentioning something about prime property, but I didn't catch any details."

Cal snorted. "I'm surprised there's anything left. He's already bought up or foreclosed on just about everything in sight. What could he be wanting now?"

"Emma, what about your place?" Matt asked, raising an eyebrow. "It's in a prime location to the railway station."

"Maybe that's what he's after," Cal suggested.

"If that's the case," Emma said, "why threaten to take Mandy away? It doesn't make sense for him to get me angry if he plans to make me another offer on my property."

"That's true," Liddy said. "And you don't owe him money, so he can't threaten to foreclose on you, like he did me."

"I sure wish I knew what that man is up to," Matt growled.

"No good, I'm sure," Cal said.

❧

Emma cleared off the last table and began to close up for the night. It had seemed natural to have Matt at the table with her and Mandy, enjoying a meal with their best friends, as if they were a family, too. It had been the most enjoyable evening she'd spent in a long time.

She carried a tray of dirty dishes to the kitchen and had just crossed the threshold when she heard a sudden cracking sound, as if a gun had gone off, followed by the shattering of glass.

"Get down, Miss Emma!" Ben yelled from the sink. He crouched, also, and they strained to listen. All was quiet. "Stay here. I'll get some help."

"I have to check on Mandy." Emma crawled to the stairs and crept up them while Ben rushed over to the telephone on the wall.

She heard him cranking it and yelling into the mouthpiece. "Operator? Are you there?"

"Get me the sheriff's office, quick," Emma heard Ben bellow as she tiptoed to the bedroom. "Sheriff? Oh, Deputy Johnson. You gotta get over here to Miss Emma's right away. Somebody shot a gun into the café!"

Emma found Mandy sleeping peacefully, a thumb in her mouth. After making sure everything was fine upstairs, she kissed the baby's head and hurried back downstairs just in time to hear Matt hollering from outside the café, "Emma! Ben! Are you all right?"

"Yes, sir, we is," Ben yelled back as he and Emma rushed to the front. One of the windowpanes in the door had been shattered, and bits of glass—large chunks, tiny shards, and everything in between—covered the floor and the tables under the window.

Matt burst through the door, his gun drawn, his boots crunching glass. After scrutinizing the room, he put the pistol back in his holster. "Is Mandy all right?"

Emma tried to sound calm. "She slept through it all."

"Was it gunfire, Deputy Matt?" Ben asked.

Matt's eyes searched the café. "I don't think so. I heard the crash from the office. It wasn't near as loud as a gunshot."

He motioned to the floor about halfway across the room. Under a chair sat a rock about the size of one of Emma's biscuits. A piece of paper was tied around it with string. Matt picked it up and released the paper. He eyed it quickly, then handed it to Emma.

The note was written on good stationery with bold handwriting. "If you know what's good for you and the town," she read aloud, "you'll give up that baby."

She blinked back tears.

"I sure don't understand some folks," Ben muttered as he began sweeping up the broken glass.

Emma was thankful the damage wasn't any worse. At least the big picture window with her café's name engraved on it remained intact.

Matt held out his hand toward Emma. "I need that note for evidence."

She handed it back to him. "I'll have to find something to put over that window until I can get the pane replaced."

"You can't stay here tonight, Emma. Whoever threw this might come back."

"I'm not going anywhere, Deputy. This is my home."

"Let me take you to Cal and Liddy's."

"No. I'm staying here. Besides, aren't you off duty?"

"I can bed down in the kitchen, Deputy," Ben said. "I'll telephone you if I hear a sound."

"I'm not leaving you here with only a telephone for protection." Matt sat at one of the tables and propped his feet up on the chair across from him. "Put on a pot of coffee, Emma. It could be a very long night."

twelve

After several uneventful hours passed, Matt finally convinced Emma to go upstairs and get some sleep so she could take care of Mandy and her business the next day. Ben chose to stay and keep Matt company, dozing off and on. Matt managed a catnap here and there but jumped at every sound.

He'd never been so frightened in his life as when Ben called and said someone had shot into Emma's café. What if it had been a gun? Or what if the rock had hit Emma in the head? He felt sick at the thought.

He thanked God that Emma and Mandy were all right, and he promised himself he'd do everything in his power to make sure they stayed that way.

❧

Emma insisted on treating Matt to breakfast before he left the next morning. She tried to give Ben the day off, but he wouldn't hear of it.

As soon as Jaffa-Prager opened, Emma sent Ben to buy a pane of glass and two door locks. She and Hallie took care of the cooking and waiting tables while Ben replaced the windowpane and installed the new locks on both the front and back doors. Emma sent up prayers of thanksgiving that God had not let anything happen to Mandy or her.

The sheriff showed up later that morning to ask questions. He assured Emma that he and his deputies would be watching her place extra closely until they found out who was responsible for throwing the rock.

Emma went through the motions of taking care of Mandy and her customers, trying not to think about the incident the night before. Matt was in and out the rest of the day. She knew it was all in the line of duty, but she did feel safer with him around.

She had to explain what happened over and over again as her customers asked about the window or begged for confirmation about the rumors they'd heard. The only other evidence left in the café was the scratched surface of her floor where the rock had skidded to a stop.

Knowing the sheriff and his deputies were right across the street, Emma slept fairly well that night.

She enjoyed the church service the next day, drawing strength from her church family. The singing raised her spirits, and the sermon reminded her that God watches over His children.

The rest of Sunday passed peacefully. Cal and Liddy repeatedly assured Emma of their faith that the Lord would not allow the town council to take Mandy away.

But when she awoke on Monday morning, Emma's heart was filled with dread. She dropped to her knees beside the bed and prayed for her faith to grow stronger, and for the Lord to give her courage to face whatever decision the council made.

Emma knew God would take care of everything. Still, she had to remind herself all day not to worry.

Business slowed down after supper, and Emma asked Hallie to close up so she could prepare for the meeting. She had just finished dressing Mandy and herself in their nicest clothes when Liddy and Cal showed up to walk with her.

She was relieved to have them at her side when they walked into the packed room. This time she saw many friendly faces in the crowd. Still, she felt intimidated as she took a seat at the front of the room and faced the councilmen seated at the table. The same men who were absent before were still out of town. Matt had taken up his post at the back of the room with the sheriff. Deputy Carmichael manned the side door.

Harper had to tap the gavel several times before the crowd quieted down enough for the meeting to get under way.

When the crowd was finally silenced, Harper explained, "for the benefit of those who weren't in attendance at the last meeting," that the council had decided to check with the orphanage in Santa Fe about taking custody of Annie's child, even though Miss Emma Hanson opposed that course of action.

"We have heard back from Santa Fe," he said, bringing them all up to date. "The orphanage director says they are willing to accept the child if we can get her there. They would prefer to have a couple from here adopt her, but no one has come forward. So the next step is to find someone willing to accompany the child to—"

"May I address the council, Mr. Harper?" Emma asked as sweetly as she could without choking.

Harper frowned at her. "After I finish, Miss Hanson."

"Let her talk," a man from the back of the room yelled.

"Yes, Harper," Doc Bradshaw said. "We want to hear what she has to say."

Color crept up the banker's neck. "Very well, Miss Hanson. You may speak your mind."

Emma faced the crowded room, holding Mandy close. "I would like to request that the council rethink this course of action, especially since I—"

"There is no reason for us to *rethink* anything."

Emma whirled around to face Harper. "But I've taken your suggestion, and I need a little more time to pursue it."

Harper spread a pudgy hand over his chest. "My suggestion? I gave you no suggestion, Miss Hanson."

"Oh, but you did," Emma said. "And I decided to heed your advice."

Harper twisted the neck of his shirt collar. "My advice?"

"Yes. Remember that day in my café? You advised me to find a mail-order husband."

The room instantly filled with titters, guffaws, and murmurs.

Harper's cheeks flushed. "Why, I never said anything of the sort."

"Oh, yes, you did," Myrtle chimed in. "I was there."

"Me, too," Opal added.

Harper turned even redder. "But I–I—"

"You didn't think I'd go through with it, did you? Well, I have. I just need some time to—"

"Did you really suggest that, Harper?" Homer Williams asked, his eyes wide.

"Well. . .uh, I might have mentioned it—"

"Then we must give Miss Hanson some time to try to carry out that plan," Homer said.

Harper looked like he might explode. "But—"

Cal stood. "If it was your suggestion, Harper, you don't have much choice other than to give her some time to follow up on it."

"Councilman," Homer Williams said, "I believe we need to talk."

Harper strode to the table. Homer and the other council members huddled around him, whispering and gesturing toward Emma for several moments. Then Homer addressed her. "You have two weeks to show us some progress in this endeavor. We will reevaluate the situation at that time."

Two weeks wasn't very long. But Emma was glad for even a temporary reprieve. "Thank you, Mr. Williams."

Matt stepped forward. "You shouldn't have to reevaluate the situation at all."

Emma's heart stopped. What was he doing?

"Mandy has been well taken care of. If any woman is capable of raising a child by herself, it's Emma Hanson. You need to drop this whole thing and let her keep the promise she made to Annie Drake."

Emma's heart began to beat again. In double-time. Matt actually thought she could raise Mandy. He was taking her side! *Thank You, Lord.*

Harper glared at Matt. "Deputy, I don't believe this is in your line of duty."

"I'm off duty, Councilman. I speak as a private citizen who has closely observed Miss Hanson—"

"Mr. Johnson, the matter has been settled." Harper pounded the gavel on the podium. "Miss Hanson has two weeks. This meeting is dismissed!"

Mandy clapped. Liddy giggled and hugged them both. Emma blinked quickly. She wasn't going to let Harper see her cry. Two weeks! How was she ever going to find a suitable husband in two weeks?

The councilmen disappeared out the side door. Emma took a shaky breath as Doc and Myrtle came over to wish her well.

"It's going to be all right, Dear," Myrtle said as Minister Turley and Caroline came over to give their support. It was wonderful to have their encouragement. But would this reprieve actually do any good?

As the crowd began to thin out, Emma, Liddy, and Cal started up the aisle. Emma searched the room for Matt but didn't see him anywhere.

"Emma, you have some time to work with," Liddy assured her. "God is going to take care of everything; just you wait and see."

"Maybe He's telling me to get out of town."

"What?"

Emma stopped in the middle of the aisle and faced her friend. "Liddy, if I can't find a husband in two weeks, I'll have no choice but to board up my business and leave town with Mandy."

"Oh, Em. You can't mean that."

"I know God wants me to keep my promise. And if it means starting over somewhere else, then I'll go."

"It won't come to that. You'll see." Liddy hugged her. "It's going to be real interesting to see how God takes care of this."

"Yes, it is," Emma said. In an attempt to lighten the somber mood, she tickled Mandy and made her giggle. "Let's go to the café and celebrate."

The café remained closed while the three friends enjoyed chocolate cake and milk together. After the McAllisters left and Mandy was safely tucked into bed, Emma brought out her packet of letters and went through them to see if there were any she could possibly reply to. She reread them all once more and put two to the side. She'd answer them and see where it led. But she didn't hold out much hope.

It seemed the Lord was leading her away from this town she loved so much. If that was His will, then that's what she'd do. Ben could run the café. He might even want to buy it.

Emma quickly penned two letters, identical except for the salutation, and stuffed them into envelopes. She retired early that night, thankful that she had some time to figure out what the Lord had in store for her. And grateful for her friends who supported her. Her heart soared as she remembered the way Matt had stood up for her. But the town council still did not believe she could raise Mandy alone.

Dear Lord, please show me what You would have me do.

⁂

Matt paced the floor of his room at the boardinghouse. The tightness in his chest had returned, more painful than ever. It had started when he overheard Emma tell Liddy that she would leave Roswell with Mandy if she had no other options. Not that he blamed her. What choice had the council given her? To marry a complete stranger or give up the child she loved? To his way of thinking, neither was acceptable.

He went to the sheriff's office and talked to Deputy Carmichael for awhile. When it came time for rounds, Matt asked him to take his shift so he could stay and keep an eye on Emma's place. After Carmichael left, Matt made himself comfortable in a chair near the open front door.

It was a quiet night, with a lot of time to think. And the longer he thought, the more clear everything became. There was no use denying it. Matt loved Emma Hanson and the baby she'd agreed to raise. Yes, he was in a dangerous business, and there was a chance he might leave her a widow. But he hated the idea of someone else marrying Emma and being a father to Mandy. And he couldn't stand the thought that she might leave the area forever. She couldn't continue living alone above the café with rock-throwing people out on the streets. Yet the thought of some other man protecting them was unacceptable.

There was only one thing to do. And he had to do it before she agreed to marry one of those letter-writers! Matt stood, straightened his shoulders, pressed his Stetson onto his head, and strode out the door. He'd march over to the café that minute and ask Emma Hanson to marry him without delay.

But as he crossed the street, he noticed the lights were out, even upstairs. Matt stopped in the middle of the road and stared at the dark building. He yanked his hat off his head and ran his fingers through his hair. Then he slammed the hat back on and strode back to the sheriff's office. Morning couldn't come soon enough.

❧

After a restless night, Emma rose just after dawn. She padded down to the kitchen to begin her preparations for the day. She'd just put on a fresh pot of coffee when a knock on the back door made her jump. Who would be calling at this hour?

She opened the door a crack and let out a gasp when she saw Matt there, his clothes wrinkled and his hair mussed.

"Emma, can we talk?" he said, his voice hoarse.

"Of course." She opened the door wider. "Is anything wrong?"

"No," he said, crossing to his usual table. "I just wanted to ask you something."

Emma poured two cups of coffee. "I've been wanting to thank you for standing up for me last night," she said as she sat across the table from him. "I tried to find you after the meeting, but you'd already gone."

Matt rubbed the sides of his coffee cup. "I overheard you tell Liddy you might leave town if you don't find. . ." His voice trailed off.

"A husband? Well, I have to do something. I won't let them

take Mandy away from me. And you can't arrest me for thinking about leaving town."

"No." Matt stared at the steaming coffee. "Could I have some milk?"

"Of course," she said more softly, regretting her sharp tone. She took a small pitcher out of the icebox and poured him a glass.

He took a small sip. "Emma, I came to ask you. . .I mean, I came to tell you that. . .there's no need for you to try to find a husband. I'll marry you."

Emma's mouth dropped open. She tried to shut it, but it refused to cooperate. Surely she hadn't heard him right. She thought he'd just said he would marry her!

His weary gaze met hers as he waited for an answer.

"Matt, I–I don't know what to say."

"Say yes. There's no need for you to marry a stranger. At least you know me. And so does Mandy. I'd be good to you and the baby. I could keep you both safe."

Emma wanted to cry. Deputy Matthew Johnson had finally asked her to marry him! Oh, how she'd ached to hear those words. But she wanted him to propose out of love, not because he pitied her. He was offering her the one thing she'd dreamed about for two long years. Yet she heard herself whisper, "No."

He blinked at her. "No?"

The shock on his face caused anger to rise in her throat. Obviously, he had expected her to fall into his arms and accept his mercy offering without hesitation. "You heard me, Deputy," she said evenly. "You have never shown any romantic interest in me before. I refuse to marry a man out of pity."

Matt reached for her hand. "It's not pity I feel for you, Emma."

"No?" She pulled her hand away from his. "Then why didn't you ask me to marry you when the council first tried to take Mandy away?"

Matt took a deep breath. "I never intended to ask anyone to marry me. I didn't want to take the chance of leaving a widow behind, like my father did. I know how hard his death was on my mother, and I promised myself I'd never do that to a woman."

Emma's heart went out to him. "I'm sure your mother was glad for every moment she had with your father because she loved him. People in love take those kinds of chances." She would gladly have taken the chance with Matthew Johnson. Everything in her cried out for her to accept his offer of marriage. But she couldn't. He didn't love her.

"Emma, if you marry me, the town council—"

Her back stiffened. "If you'd asked me to marry you a year ago, or even several months ago, I would have said yes."

His eyes widened with hope. "Really?"

"But if you really cared for me, you would have shown it before now. I cannot marry a man who simply pities me." Emma rose and opened the back door. "I do appreciate your kind offer, Deputy."

"Emma—"

"But I need to go check on Mandy now."

Matt took a deep breath. "All right." He stood before her, close enough for her to see the hurt and confusion in his eyes. . . which almost made her melt into his arms. She steeled herself.

"If you change your mind—"

"I'll let you see yourself out." Emma scurried up the stairs. She couldn't let him see her cry.

❧

Matt stood alone in the kitchen, wondering what he'd done wrong. Asking Emma to marry him had seemed the answer to her problem as well as his. But somehow he'd messed things up, and he had no idea how to fix it.

The thought had never crossed his mind that Emma might turn him down. She was willing to marry a complete stranger, but she wouldn't marry him? It made no sense!

As he stood there, gazing up the stairs, he vaguely heard a man's voice behind him. "Deputy Matt? Is ever'thin' all right with Miss Emma?"

Matt shook himself out of his stupor and saw Ben giving him a quizzical look. "What? Oh, yes. She's fine. She went to check on Mandy. I was just on my way out."

"Want me to fix you some flapjacks?"

"No, thanks. I'm not very hungry this morning." Matt wandered out the door, wondering if he'd ever be hungry again.

Emma was beautiful first thing in the morning. He'd never seen her hair long, the soft tresses curling around her face and down her back. His fingers had fairly itched to be able to run through those curls.

He walked down the boardwalk, with no particular destination in mind, finally ending up at the livery stable. This was certainly not the way he'd planned to spend his day off when he spent the night on the stoop outside the sheriff's office, waiting for the first sign of activity in the café.

Matt saddled his horse and headed out toward Cal and Liddy's. Maybe they could make some sense of this.

The McAllisters were just finishing breakfast when he reined up outside their house. The girls ran out to do their chores before school, and Liddy insisted on setting him a place and filling a plate with bacon and biscuits and gravy. He tried to eat, but the food just wasn't going down.

Cal let him sit in silence for a few minutes, then asked, "What's wrong, Matt? You look like you've lost your best friend."

Matt realized he might well have. "I asked Emma to marry me."

Liddy jumped up and hugged his neck. "I was hoping you would! When's the date?"

"She turned me down." His stomach felt like it was on fire.

Liddy sank back into her chair. "She did what?"

"She told me no. Said she didn't want my pity." Matt shook his head. "It's not pity I feel for her."

"Well, did you tell her that?" Cal asked.

"I tried to. She wouldn't listen. She said if I'd asked her a year ago. . .even a few months ago. . ."

"Well, she has been sweet on you for the longest time." Liddy rested her chin in her hand.

"That's not true."

"If you believe that, you haven't been paying attention. I'm her best friend. Believe me, I know. She's been interested in you since before Cal and I fell in love."

Matt slapped his hand on the table. "Then why didn't she ever show it?"

"Oh, she did." Liddy exchanged glances with Cal, then settled her attention back on Matt. "Remember right after you moved here? Didn't Emma bring you supper a few times when you were working?"

"Well, yes, but I—"

"But you insisted on paying her. Claimed you didn't want to be beholden to anyone."

"So?"

"So she took that to mean you weren't interested in her."

Matt groaned. "I never intended to marry anyone."

"What made you change your mind?" Cal asked.

Matt pushed his chair back and started pacing. "I can't stand the fact that she might marry a stranger, or that she might leave town. I love her." At that instant, Matt realized that he'd never said those words to Emma. No wonder she'd turned him down!

Cal grinned. "About time you figured that out. So, what are you going to do now?"

"You aren't giving up, are you?" Liddy asked.

"I don't know what to do. She won't listen to me right now."

"Can you write?" Liddy cocked an eyebrow at him.

"Of course I can."

"And Emma can read. Matter of fact, she's been reading a lot lately." Liddy grinned at him. "Letters, mostly."

Cal laughed. "I think I know where you're going with this."

For the first time that day, Matt smiled. "I think I do, too."

thirteen

Emma managed to hold her tears at bay while she waited on her customers. But after the café closed, Ben went home, and Mandy fell asleep, she couldn't keep them in check any longer.

She sobbed into her pillow, hoping she wouldn't wake the baby. Her heart ached for what could have been. If only Matt had asked her to marry him earlier, even a couple of months ago, before the first town council meeting about Mandy.

She'd loved Matt for such a long time. She knew he'd make a wonderful husband and father. Even after waiting so long, this day could have ended joyfully. . .if only he'd said those three words she longed to hear.

But he hadn't. As difficult as it would be to marry a stranger, at least they'd be starting out with the intention of learning to love each other. The idea of marrying a man she loved, but who felt nothing for her but pity, was too painful to even think about. No. As much as she wanted to say yes, she couldn't marry Matt, knowing he didn't love her.

Emma's chest heaved with silent tears long into the night, until she finally gave it over to the Lord. She prayed He would guide her in choosing a husband from the letters she'd received. Then she asked God to help her get over Matt so she could learn to love another.

Early the next morning, Mandy's sweet voice woke her. "Em-mama, I hungry."

Emma felt drained but at peace. The Lord had given her this precious child to raise as her own. He would help her—whether by sending a good man to marry her or by enabling her to relocate. He was in control. She would leave everything in His hands.

Emma washed her face and peered into the mirror. Her eyes looked a little swollen from all the crying, but they weren't red. She dressed herself and Mandy and slipped downstairs.

All in all, she thought she was doing quite well. . .until Liddy came in with the pies and cakes. She took one look at Emma and said, "Matt doesn't look much better than you do."

Emma teared up again.

"I'm sorry, Em," Liddy said. "I didn't mean to make you cry." She gave Emma a tight hug. Then she held her at arm's length and gazed into her bleary eyes. "Now, what is this I hear about you turning down that man's proposal? I thought it was what you've been waiting for."

"Liddy, I wanted him to love me." Emma wiped her eyes with a dish towel.

"And how do you know he doesn't?"

She sniffed. "I gave him plenty of opportunity to say so."

"Those words don't come easy for some men."

Emma began feeding Mandy her breakfast. "Liddy, I've got to trust the Lord to bring someone into my life who is at least willing to try to love me." She wished with all her heart that things could be different, but she couldn't daydream about Matt for the rest of her life. "Last night I wrote two letters of response to the men who answered my advertisement."

Liddy opened her mouth as if to say something, then shut it. "Would you like me to walk to the post office with you?"

"Thanks for understanding, Liddy. Would you mind

putting Mandy in her carriage while I run upstairs and get those letters?"

"Not at all."

Liddy and Mandy were ready to go when Emma came back down, the two letters tucked into her skirt pocket. Emma asked Ben to watch the café for awhile.

At the post office, Emma handed her letters to Mr. Marley, and he gave her another envelope. The return address showed no name, only a post office box right there in Roswell.

She had specifically decided not to place an ad in the local paper, and she'd asked Matt not to spread word around town. Yet somehow, someone had found out!

Emma glanced up at Mr. Marley, sorely tempted to ask him who owned the box marked on the envelope. But she knew he wouldn't be allowed to give out that information. So she kept the question to herself.

"Well?" Liddy asked, watching Emma stuff the unopened envelope in her skirt pocket. "Aren't you going to read it?"

Emma chuckled at her friend's impatience. "Later."

"Aw, Em, I have an interest in this, too. I don't want you moving away. Maybe I can help by giving you an impartial opinion on some of these men."

Emma handed her the letter. "All right. You read it first and tell me what you think."

Liddy gave it back. "No, no. I just want to read the ones you think you might want to answer."

Emma held the letter as they strolled back to the café. "I doubt there will be anything different in these letters than what I've read in all the others. But, like you said, maybe an objective eye will see more than I would."

When they returned to the café, Emma invited Liddy in

for a cup of tea. As she settled Mandy in the play area, she watched Ben taking care of the cooking and waiting on customers. He didn't seem to have any problem handling both jobs. He ought to own his own place. Perhaps she really would sell him the café if she had to move.

Hallie came in for work, and Emma ran upstairs to get the packet of letters so Liddy could go over all of them.

When she came back down, she saw Liddy at the kitchen table, sipping tea. Emma dropped the packet on the table along with the new letter. "You might as well check them all out. Maybe you'll see something I missed."

Emma took out several orders and refilled coffee cups, then joined her friend in the kitchen. "Well?"

Liddy pushed several letters toward her. "I'd burn these. My goodness, Emma, I didn't realize there were so many men out there wanting a free meal ticket."

Emma laughed. "I'm glad I didn't let all their sweet talking mislead me."

"Sweet talking? One of these men asked right out if your business could support his family. Another one expects you to sign your business over to him before marriage. What nerve!"

Emma picked up one of the letters and waved it in the air. "What about the one who wants me to move to the top of a mountain, where there are no neighbors for miles around? You know I couldn't do that. I'm too used to having people around me every day."

Liddy took a sip of her tea. "Are you sure it was such a good idea refusing Matt's offer of marriage? It's not like you've received any wonderful responses to that advertisement."

Emma stood. "You don't have to read the rest." Emma

reached for the letters. "You've confirmed that my instincts are accurate."

"Why don't I just read one more?" She held up the letter Emma had just picked up that morning.

Emma snatched it out of her hand. "I'll save this one for later," she said, deciding she'd rather be the first one to read it.

Liddy nodded. "All right. But don't give up hope. God is going to take care of all this."

"I know. I've already decided where I might go if I decide to leave."

"I don't want to hear about you moving." Liddy stood. "I'm not even going to discuss it with you."

Emma didn't want to talk about it, either. But she had to be prepared, and a plan was forming in the back of her mind. Matt had complained about the food at the restaurant in the Lincoln Hotel. If the council tried to take Mandy away, maybe Emma would set up business there. It wasn't far away, so she could easily come back to Roswell from time to time to visit her friends.

Liddy waved good-bye as Emma turned her attention to her customers.

During a lull in the early evening, Emma pulled the new envelope out of her skirt pocket. She opened the folded sheet of paper and read.

Dear Miss Hanson,

I put pen to paper not knowing quite what to say because I have never done this kind of thing before. But somehow I do not think you make a habit of advertising for a husband, either. I never thought much about getting married until recently. But lately I have been yearning for a home and a family of my own.

Emma's attention was caught. She sat in the nearest chair to give this intriguing letter her undivided attention.

Allow me to tell you a little about myself. I do like children, very much. How many children would you want?

Emma blushed. She realized she hadn't made it clear in the advertisement that there already was a child. She wondered why none of the other men had mentioned that.

I have a steady job, so I would not be needing your business to support us or any children we might have, although if you wished to keep your place of business, that would be all right with me.

Emma placed a hand over her heart. This was the first letter she'd received where the man had voiced a willingness to provide for her and any children involved. The paper shook as her hand began to tremble.

I do not drink, and I am a God-fearing man. . .although there have been times in my life when I did not lean on the Lord as I should have and forged ahead on my own. I am now trying to let Him lead me into the future.

Tears formed in Emma's eyes. It seemed she had something in common with this man right off the bat. Trying to be in charge, when they knew the only way things worked out was to seek God's will in the way they should go

I would not expect you to make a decision on one letter alone. Therefore, I would like very much to correspond with you, should you be so inclined, so that we might get to know each other well enough to reach the decision the Lord would have us make.

I hope to hear from you in the near future.

Sincerely,
DMJ

She wondered why he signed only his initials. She thought of all the men she knew, but no names matched.

Emma reread the letter, her heart pounding with hope. Could this be the one she was to answer? Was this the man the Lord was sending to her and Mandy?

❧

Matt stood across from Emma's café trying to summon up the courage to cross the street and go in. He hadn't seen her since she'd turned down his proposal, and he wasn't sure how she would react to him behaving as if nothing had happened between them. But that's exactly what he intended to do. He didn't want to give her any hint of what his plan of action was.

Thanks to Cal and Liddy, he wasn't giving up. Not yet. He'd thought about everything Liddy had told him about Emma's feelings for him.

Although Emma seemed convinced that all he felt for her was pity, she couldn't be further from the truth. But she wouldn't listen to what he had to say, and even if she did, Matt wasn't sure he could change her mind. Still, if she did care for him at one time, could she not care again? And if she was willing to consider a suitor by mail, why not see if she would consider him? It seemed to be his only chance.

He'd penned the letter at Cal and Liddy's house and put it in the mail that afternoon. He wondered if Emma would answer it. In the meantime, he couldn't stay away from her place. It was his job to make sure no one caused problems, especially after the council meeting. Harper and several of his cronies had been quite angry. They hadn't wanted to give her any extra time to find a husband. Matt was determined to make sure they gave Emma those two weeks as promised.

Matt had a job to do. He crossed the street and entered the café, taking a seat at his regular table. The place was busy and he was glad for that. It would make things easier on both him and Emma.

She stopped by his table and set down a glass of water. "What can I get for you tonight, Deputy?"

"Whatever the special is will be fine, thank you." He gazed into her eyes for a brief moment before she blinked and headed for the kitchen.

Matt rubbed his hands on his pant legs and let out a deep breath. That hadn't been too bad. At least she hadn't told him to go away. He'd noticed dark circles under her eyes. Matt wished with all his heart that he could take her in his arms and assure her that everything would be all right. But he didn't have that right. If she didn't reply to his letter, he might never have it.

Matt also wanted to check on Mandy but figured he'd better bide his time.

He ate his meal in silence, missing the easy conversation he had once shared with Emma and now realized he'd taken for granted. He'd been content to see her several times a day, knowing there was no love interest in her life, assuring himself that she wouldn't be attracted to someone in his line of work and figuring he was doing her a favor by not pursuing her.

If she had cared about him, as Liddy indicated, he must have seemed callous and uncaring. Why should Emma have taken his proposal seriously? He had never given her a reason to believe that he felt anything but friendship for her.

No wonder she thought he felt only pity for her. He'd been too busy telling himself he was doing the proper thing by not acting on his attraction to her, by not showing her how much he cared.

Matt bowed his head over his food, and right there in Emma's café, he said a silent prayer. *Dear God, forgive me for my self-righteousness and arrogance. Please let Emma forgive me, Father. If I should be so blessed to persuade her to marry me, help me to spend the rest of my life making it up to her. In Jesus' name, amen.*

⁂

Emma breathed a sigh of relief when she let the last customer out and locked up for the night. She cleared off their table on her way back to the kitchen to help Ben with the cleanup, eager to reread the letter in her pocket.

She knew the only way she'd been able to handle waiting on Matt was thinking about that letter. That made it easier to face his pity.

She nearly pushed Ben out the door, assuring him she'd finish the preparations for the next day. Once alone, she brewed a pot of tea and sat at the kitchen table. She pulled out the letter and read it once more and then again. It was like a balm to her battered pride, and she knew she was going to answer this one. And she certainly wasn't going to hand it over to the sheriff to check out.

She gathered paper and pen and mulled over how to start.

She dipped her pen in the ink and wrote.

Dear DMJ,

I must admit I am curious as to why you used initials instead of your full name. Might I ask the reason?

You are right; I do not make it a habit of advertising for a husband, and I feel awkward about doing it. But truthfully, I felt I did not have a choice. You have been straightforward with me, and now I feel you should know why I have done this, so that you can decide if you would like to continue corresponding with me.

You see, I have been given the opportunity to be a mother to the most wonderful child in the world. A woman who worked for me died, after extracting a promise that I would raise her daughter. Even if I had not fallen in love with this baby, I would have kept my promise to Annie. I feel honored that she trusted me enough to put her child in my care.

But the leaders of this town do not feel a single woman should be raising a child, and they have given me a deadline of two weeks to find a husband. If I do not find the right man by then, I will take my child and find a new place to live before they can take her away from me and place her in an orphanage.

If, after hearing all of this, you feel led to reply to me, I will answer in kind.

Sincerely,
Emma Hanson

Emma folded the paper and slid it into an envelope, addressing it to the post office box of the sender. She propped it against the lamp on the table and let out a shaky breath. It would go out in the mail first thing the next morning.

She felt an unexplainable peace about answering this man. She was certain it came from the Lord, and she was going to put her faith in Him. If she shouldn't feel that way, He would let her know. Until then, she would wait impatiently for a reply.

fourteen

Before he started his shift, Matt checked in at the post office. When Mr. Marley handed him a letter bearing Emma's return address, Matt tried not to show his excitement. His first thought was to tear into it immediately, but there were other people in the post office, and he wanted privacy when he read Emma's letter.

After work, he'd go home and read it. He folded it carefully and put it in his pants pocket. She'd actually replied to his letter. Whatever she wrote, it would be more than the cool remarks he'd received the last couple of days. Would Emma ever really talk to him again? He missed having conversations with her, missed her smile, missed feeling comfortable enough to walk into the kitchen and check on Mandy. If Emma's letter asked him not to write again, he didn't know what his next move would be. But he wasn't going to give up until he had the chance to convince her how much he cared about her and that little girl.

He loved them—plain and simple. He should have told Emma that the morning he proposed. But her refusal had made him realize how much he needed her and Mandy in his life, probably more than they needed him.

He walked out of the post office with a spring in his step. He knew it wasn't fair of him to write her anonymously and only include his post office box, but she probably wouldn't have read his letter if she'd known it was from him. He was

hoping she might begin to care about him through their correspondence. At least he would have a chance to convince her
that he loved her and truly did want to marry her.

It was all he could do to keep from tearing into the envelope
while at work, and as soon as his shift was over, he hurried
back to the boardinghouse and sat at the desk in his room.

Matt smoothed out the page and scanned the words. Emma
had opened the door for him to correspond with her. He let
out the breath he'd been holding and smiled. She was being
honest with someone she thought was a complete stranger.

She asked about his initials, obviously wanting to know his
name. He couldn't tell her yet—it would end it all immediately.
He felt some guilt that he wasn't being completely honest with
her. But he would be. Just as soon as he thought he could.

He immediately began composing an answer. With the
town council's two-week deadline, there was no time to lose.

Dear Miss Hanson,

*I am pleased that you have agreed to correspond with
me. Thank you for letting me know why you thought you
must advertise for a husband. I think your young charge
is fortunate to be in the care of someone who cares so
much about her well-being.*

*I am looking forward to meeting you both one day.
I would consider it an honor to help you raise her for
her mother.*

*I will be glad to meet with you in person whenever and
wherever you say. I understand the time limit imposed on
you by your town leaders, so I will leave it up to you on
how to proceed. I confess to having admired you from
afar for some time now, so I would not have to travel a*

*long distance to meet with you. Just set the time and
place, and I will be there.*

Sincerely,
DMJ

Matt folded the paper and stuffed it in an envelope. He strolled over to the post office and dropped it in the after-hours door slot. He figured Emma would receive it the next day.

28.

Emma felt giddy with excitement when she opened the letter she'd brought back from the post office. She scanned it quickly, as she had customers who needed her attention, but her stomach did flips at the knowledge that "DMJ" wanted to continue the correspondence. Since he lived in the area, she wondered if she'd met him before.

She knew she should be cautious in this correspondence with a stranger, but she felt peace about it, a peace she hadn't felt with any of the other letters. She was going to proceed and trust in the Lord to show her if she was wrong.

When Liddy came in that morning, Emma decided to tell her about this new man over a cup of coffee.

"Well, I finally answered one of the men who responded to my advertisement," she began.

"Oh?" Liddy's cup stalled midway to her lips.

"The last one I received was. . .different from the others." Emma twirled her cup in its saucer.

Liddy leaned in. "What did it say? Who was it from?"

Emma handed both envelopes to Liddy. She'd carried the first letter in her pocket from the first day and read it countless times. She knew she'd do the same with the one she'd received that morning.

Liddy quickly read both letters and grinned at Emma. "Oh, my. He sounds awfully nice. I think you did the right thing by replying to him."

"I do, too."

Liddy pursed her lips together. "When are you going to meet this man?"

Emma shrugged. "I haven't decided yet. Apparently he knows me, which puts me at a disadvantage."

"Did you give these envelopes to the sheriff or Matt to check out?"

"No. I don't want them knowing my business."

Liddy shrugged. "I guess I might feel the same way. Still. . ."

Emma grinned. "I'm trusting in the Lord, Liddy."

"Then it's bound to turn out right."

"That's what I think." Emma took a sip of coffee and sat back in her chair.

"Have you talked to Matt since he proposed?" Liddy asked, handing the letters back to Emma.

"He's been in a few times, but it's hard to go back to the way things were. I'll always care about him. But I have to get over him." She put the letters back in her pocket. "These are helping keep my mind off of him, and that's a good thing."

"If you say so." Liddy stood. "I'd better be going. I need to get some cocoa. The girls have been wanting hot chocolate."

"It is getting cooler. Especially at night." Emma cleared the table. "Hot chocolate sounds good to me. My customers will be asking for it before long. I'd better see about getting some cocoa for the café."

She hugged her friend good-bye, then patted her pocket as she returned to the kitchen. Maybe there'd be someone in her life to share a cup of cocoa with by wintertime. After Liddy's departure, there was no one else in the café, so Emma pulled out her writing supplies. She wanted to get her reply to the post office before she got too busy.

❧

When Matt came in for an early supper that evening, he saw Emma standing at the counter, reading a letter. The bell above the door jingled when he entered, and she glanced up with a smile. But as soon as she saw him, the smile faded.

He caught a glimpse of the letter as she stuffed it into her pocket, and Matt almost chuckled as he recognized his own handwriting.

He knew Emma was going to be angry when she found out that he was the one writing those letters. And the day of reckoning was soon approaching. It was only a matter of time until they met in person.

Dear Lord, please let Emma care. Give me the words to convince her that I love her.

He didn't see her smile again that night. But he was comforted to see her slip her hand into the pocket holding his letter. His heart thudded with hope.

❧

The next day, Matt sat two rows back from Emma and Mandy in church, trying to keep his mind on the service instead of the way Mandy grinned at him from over Emma's shoulder. *Oh, Lord, please let this work out. I want so much to be a good husband to Emma and father to Mandy. I don't want to even consider that any other man might fill those roles.*

The day passed slowly for Matt. Emma and Mandy went to Cal and Liddy's for Sunday dinner. He knew the couple was hoping for things to work out between him and Emma, but now wasn't the time for him to show up unexpectedly. Anxious for the day to end so he could pick up his mail the next morning, he offered to take Deputy Carmichael's shift so the young man could go visit a lady he'd been courting.

The sun was setting when Matt saw Emma and Mandy returned to town. Only then did he relax, knowing they were home safe. While he thought it was a good thing that Emma's café was closed on Sundays, he missed the opportunity to see her. If things worked out the way he hoped and prayed they would, he'd be seeing Emma and Mandy every day. He cast an eye heavenward and felt a sudden peace about it all. God was in control, and everything was going to be all right.

It had taken him a long time to come to that conclusion. For years he'd blamed the Lord for his father's death and his mother's hard life. But it was an outlaw who killed his father. His father had loved his job, and his mother had loved him. She never blamed God for her husband's death.

That night, as he started his last rounds, Matt saw the light still on in Emma's upstairs apartment. He wondered if she'd answered his letter yet. Would she agree to a time and place to meet? He wanted this charade to end as soon as possible.

He headed to the south end of Main Street, glad that it was a quiet night in Roswell. The saloons were closed on Sundays, for which Matt was grateful. He greeted several couples out for an evening stroll and hoped that one day he and Emma would be doing the same thing.

He sauntered back up the street, checking locks and peering into windows. When he neared the café, he noticed Emma's light was off. She must have gone to bed.

But as he came closer, he realized things weren't as peaceful as they seemed. His nostrils flared when they picked up the acrid smell of something burning. He couldn't see any smoke, but he started running toward Emma's. When he rounded the corner of her building, he saw flames. They seemed to be coming from a pile of rubbish outside her kitchen door.

Matt banged on the door. "Emma! Wake up!"

He kicked dirt at the growing fire and yelled again. "Emma!"

The flames began licking the side of the wall. Matt backed up and ran toward the door, slamming against it with his shoulder. A piercing pain shot through his arm, but the door didn't budge. "Emma!"

He stepped back to try again just as Ben came running from around the front of the building. Matt heard the clang of the fire engine in the distance.

"Help is comin'," Ben said.

Matt rammed into the door with his other shoulder, and it gave way with a crack. Matt ran in and met Emma on the stairs, Mandy in her arms.

"What's burning? What's going on?"

Matt grabbed her and pulled her and the baby through the doorway. He rushed them out into the alley just as the firemen arrived and began to douse the flames. Two firemen manned the hand pumps on either side of the wagon, filling the hose from the water tank, while two others directed the hose at the fire.

Emma's hand came to her mouth. "How did this happen? I don't remember leaving anything on the stove."

"This is not your fault," Matt assured her. "The stove is nowhere near the fire. Those flames started on the outside wall, not inside."

"Who would do such a thing?"

Matt's arms encircled the two most important people in his life, and he sent up a prayer of thanksgiving that they were all right. Taking a deep breath, he fought for composure and shook his head. "I don't know. But I intend to find out who's behind this, no matter how long it takes."

❧

Emma felt chilled when Matt released his hold on her and Mandy. He sent Ben to awaken the sheriff, then started scouring the alley for clues. When Ben returned with Sheriff Haynes, the two men assisted in the search.

Emma was grateful that the outside wall to the café was only scorched, thanks to Ben's quick action. Once the fire was out, the fire marshal brought everyone inside and began asking questions.

"I saw a man run off from here a few minutes ago," Ben said, "just before the flames started up. I ran to the fire station right away to get help, so I didn't get a good look at his face."

Mandy fell back to sleep amid all the chaos, and Emma put her down in her little corner in the kitchen. She put on some coffee for the men, listening attentively to their conversation.

Her hands shook as she poured several cups. First the rock and now this. Was someone trying to frighten her? If so, he was doing a very good job. Emma sent a prayer heavenward, thanking God for putting Ben and Matt in the right place at the right time, grateful that they had worked so quickly to send for help and to get her and Mandy out.

She asked Ben to start breakfast for the men, then went back outside to inspect the damage. Her mind filled with the memory of how comforting it had felt to be held snugly in Matt's arms as he pulled her and Mandy out of harm's way. Never in her life had she felt so safe and protected. She shook that thought out of her mind, sternly reminding herself that the deputy was only doing his duty. Besides, what was she doing daydreaming when she had such a huge mess to clean up?

&

Matt's heart still hammered in his chest hours after the fire was put out. Over and over again, he thanked the Lord that Emma and Mandy were all right. If anything had happened to Emma and the baby—

"Son, we're going to find out who did this." The sheriff slapped Matt's back as they walked to the office after eating the large breakfast Emma had served them.

"I know. I wish we'd found something in that alley to point to who did it. I have a few suspicions, though. I think we should start by having a talk with Jed Brewster."

"I had the same idea. I also think we should double the watch on her place."

"Sounds good to me," Matt said.

"Why don't you go on home and get some rest, Son?" Sheriff Haynes suggested.

Matt went home, but he didn't rest. First thing in the morning, he got cleaned up and hurried over to the post office. His fatigue disappeared when he saw he had a letter from Emma.

Tearing open the envelope as soon as he got outside, he scanned the letter quickly. One line stood out.

Because time is of importance, would it be possible for us to meet this coming Wednesday, at my café, at 9 P.M.?"

Matt almost let out a whoop of joy right there in the street.

He sat down on a bench outside the post office and composed a response. It was time to tell her the truth. That he was the one writing the letters. And that he loved her with all his heart.

fifteen

Monday felt two days long. With so little sleep and so much going on, Emma had little time to wonder if "DMJ" had received her letter suggesting they meet on Wednesday evening.

Ben boarded up the back wall as best he could until a carpenter could get there to provide an estimate on fixing the charred wood. Once word about the fire got out, Emma's café was busier than ever with customers coming in to check on her. . .after they checked out the back of her building.

When Liddy and Cal came in and heard about the fire, they tried to convince Emma to move out to Liddy's old house.

"It's been empty since Annie passed away," Cal reminded her.

"Now, what good would that do?" Emma said. "It would take the fire department twice as long to get there as here."

"You're right," Liddy said. "I just worry about you and Mandy here alone. Then again, maybe that won't be the case much longer?" Liddy asked, raising her eyebrows.

"We'll see." Emma had to admit that she would feel safer having a man around. She wanted a husband, and Mandy needed a father. While her first choice would have been Matt, he'd made no more mention of his proposal. If he really loved her, he wouldn't have taken no for an answer, would he?

She needed to keep her mind off the memory of being held by him when he rescued her and Mandy from the fire. Maybe her meeting with DMJ would put all thoughts of Matt out of her mind.

Emma thought she'd have a hard time sleeping that night, worrying if someone might come back to finish the job he'd started. But the sheriff had assured her that her place would be watched constantly until they found out who was behind the fire, and she was so exhausted she found herself drifting off to sleep almost before her head hit the pillow.

⚜

With all the work involved repairing the smoke and water damage, it was Wednesday before Emma had a chance to pick up her mail again. She brought the letter she picked up back to the café, and her fingers shook as she opened it.

He would be at the café *"promptly at nine o'clock in the evening. . .if not before."*

As she clutched the letter to her chest, Emma was certain God had sent this man into her and Mandy's life. But there was a niggling doubt about the fact that she still didn't know the man. How could this possibly work?

Then she reminded herself that there had been arranged marriages since Bible times. This wouldn't be much different, assuming DMJ actually did propose. . .would it?

The butterflies in her stomach multiplied as the day went on. Each time the bell above the door jingled, her heart skittered. She tried to keep her hair neat throughout the day, but there was no preventing the tendrils from escaping out of the bun at the top of her head and curling around her face. After supper she changed into one of her favorite dresses: a cream-and-rose-striped cotton with a deep lace yoke.

As nine o'clock drew near, Emma wondered if she should have had the sheriff check out the post office box number after all. Well, it was too late now.

A few minutes before nine, the bell jingled and Emma's heart jumped. She looked up quickly but saw only Matt. *Of course, he would pick now to show up!* She blew the escaping hairs up over her forehead and went to take his order.

"Evenin', Deputy." He did look nice, dressed in a new plaid shirt, his face freshly shaven.

"Evening, Emma." Matt sat at his table. "You and Mandy doing all right?"

"We're fine. Thanks again for helping the other night."

Matt's gaze caught hers. "You're welcome. I'm glad Ben and I were there."

The warmth in his expression reminded Emma of how it had felt to be held in his arms, and she gave herself an inward shake. She had no business thinking about Matt now. "What can I get you?"

"Just a piece of pie and glass of milk, please."

She hurried off toward the kitchen. Milk instead of coffee again, she noticed. He must still be having stomach problems. She hoped it wasn't anything more. Maybe she should suggest—

What was she thinking? Matt was a grown man. He could take care of himself. And she'd do well to quit worrying about him. He wasn't in her future.

The sudden peal of the telephone interrupted her thoughts. She scrambled to answer it, wondering who would be calling her.

She'd no sooner pressed the receiver to her ear than she heard Liddy's excited voice on the other end. "We got our telephone today."

"That's wonderful."

"So, has *he* shown up yet?" Liddy asked.

"No. But naturally, Matt did. I don't want him here when—"

Emma thought she heard her friend chuckle, but it turned into a brief coughing spell. "I have to go," Liddy said when she regained her voice. "I'll talk to you later."

"All right." Emma placed the earpiece back on its hook. She grinned at Ben as she opened the icebox. "Think we'll ever get used to the telephone ringing?"

"Not me. That sound scared about ten years off my life."

Emma laughed as she poured Matt's milk and dished up his pie. She was still grinning when she set the food on his table. But when she glanced at his face, her humor died away. Matt was smiling at her, the expression in his eyes one she'd never seen before. Her heart began to beat ferociously, and she couldn't make herself turn away from the warmth of his gaze. She swallowed hard. A moment passed. Then two.

Matt cleared his throat. "Emma. . ."

She couldn't let Matt affect her like this. In just a few minutes, she was going to meet her future husband. She had to put her feelings for Matt in the past where they belonged.

Leaving him to check on her other customers, Emma saw that the last group who remained were ready to go. She took their money and cleared the table, trying to ignore Matt and calm herself down. The wall clock's hands were inching toward nine. She flipped the OPEN sign to CLOSED but didn't lock the door. She glanced up and down the street, hoping to catch a glimpse of her future husband.

When she turned around, she saw that Matt had finished his pie and milk. "Emma, could we talk a minute?" he asked softly.

She really didn't want him here. Not now. "Matt, I really have a lot to do."

Matt leaned back in his chair. "I know. You're waiting for someone, aren't you?"

Emma stopped breathing for a moment. "How did you know? Did Cal and Liddy—?"

"Emma, I. . ."

While she waited for him to finish his sentence, Emma decided there was no reason not to tell him the truth. He'd know soon enough, anyway. "I am waiting for someone, Matt. I don't mean to be rude, but I would appreciate it if you'd leave."

He shook his head. "I'm afraid I can't do that."

Why was he being so stubborn?

Emma's heart seemed to stop when she saw him pull a letter out of his pocket. The writing looked exactly like hers.

Emma sank into the chair across from him. "Where did you get that?"

"From my post office box. Your nine o'clock appointment is with me, Emma. I'm the man you're waiting on. I'm the one who's been writing the letters you've been answering." He shrugged. "I'm DMJ."

No. This couldn't be. Emma blinked back sudden tears. "I don't know what kind of joke you're trying to play, Matthew Johnson, but it's not funny."

He reached across the table and gathered her hand in his. "It's no joke, Emma. I came here to—"

Emma jerked her hand out of his. "No! You aren't—you can't be. . ."

"Deputy Matt Johnson. DMJ." He ran his fingers through his hair. "I'm sorry for misleading you, Emma. I hope you can forgive me. But I couldn't sign my name to those letters. You would never have answered me."

"I should have known." Emma fought tears of hurt and anger. How could he pull such a cruel trick on her? He'd always been her friend, or so she'd thought. This was a terrible thing to do to a person's emotions.

Emma jumped up and pointed to the door. "Get out of here, Deputy. This instant. And don't ever come back."

Matt didn't budge. "No," he said, calmly but firmly. "I'm not going anywhere until you hear me out. Emma, I meant every word I wrote in those letters. I would be honored to be your husband and be a father to Mandy."

"We've been through this before, Matt." Emma walked to the door and held it open. "We have nothing more to talk about."

Matt got up and walked toward her. "I believe we do." He gently shut the door. "And this time you're going to listen to me. If you don't like what I have to say, you can kick me out."

He cupped her cheek in his hand. "I'm not very good with words, Emma. I didn't say all I should have when I asked you to marry me last week. I'd never done that before, and I admit to not quite knowing how to do it properlike."

Emma's chin inched upward. She blinked rapidly and bit her bottom lip. She supposed she did owe him the courtesy of listening to him.

His hand moved to her shoulder, his gaze never leaving her face. "I seem to have left out the most important part of any proposal." Matt pulled her closer. "I love you, Emma Hanson. I've loved you for a very long time. And I love Mandy, too. I want to marry you; I want to help you raise that beautiful little girl. I want to spend the rest of my life showing you both how much I mean every word I'm saying. Just give me a chance. Please."

Emma couldn't stop the tears that flowed down her cheeks. "I don't want pity from you—"

"What I feel for you is *not* pity, Emma. You are the most amazing woman I've ever known. I love you. If the town council decided right this minute to give up the fight to take Mandy away from you, I would still be asking you to marry me. Please believe me."

It was everything she'd ever hoped to hear from Deputy Matt Johnson. . .and more. She nodded, slightly at first and then vigorously. Matt's head dipped, and his lips claimed hers in precisely the way she'd dreamed they would. She returned his kiss with all the love that was in her heart.

"Miss Emma?" Ben's voice ended the kiss as he pushed open the door from the kitchen. "Oh!" he said when he saw her in Matt's embrace. "Excuse me."

Emma and Matt chuckled as Ben headed back to the kitchen, muttering, " 'Bout time, that's what I say."

"That's what I say, too." Matt's lips found hers once more and lingered there for moments marked only by heartbeats. Finally, he broke off the kiss and led her back to the table. After she sat, he bent down on one knee and took her hand in his.

"Emma Hanson, I would be honored if you would accept my proposal of marriage. I love you with all that is in me. Will you be my wife?"

Emma's heart seemed to melt into a puddle. "I would be delighted to be your wife."

Matt pulled her face to his, settling his lips on hers again. When the kiss ended, he raised his head and gazed into her eyes. "I promise you, I will find some other kind of job so you don't have to worry about becoming a widow."

She brushed at her tears. "Oh, Matt, there's no need to change professions. The Lord willing, we'll grow old together. But if not, I'll be thankful for each moment we can share. . . just as I'm sure your mother was for her time with your father."

As Matt stood, he pulled her off the chair and into the circle of his arms for another kiss. Emma silently thanked the Lord for bringing Annie into her life. From the promise she made to raise Mandy had come her heart's desire—a family of her own. . .with the man she'd always loved.

epilogue

Emma's heart sang with joy as she walked into the town council meeting the following Monday. But, at Matt and the sheriff's suggestion, she worked hard not to show it. She was doing just fine—until she glanced over to where Matt was standing, in his usual place at the back of the room. His almost imperceptible wink was nearly her undoing. Her heart pounded so hard she felt it would surely burst with all the love she felt for that man.

To keep her composure, she quickly glanced the other way and continued up the aisle with Mandy on her hip, Cal and Liddy following behind. They took their seats in the front row and waited for the meeting to come to order. The same men were seated at the table in the front of the room.

From the smirk on Harper's face as he sat at the table with the other councilmen, it was obvious he thought he'd won. Emma couldn't wait for him to find out what was in store for him.

He took out his pocket watch and examined it, then put it back and stood. "Ladies and gentlemen, it's time to call the meeting to order. The main issue of business tonight is finding a permanent home for the Drake child. The orphanage in Santa Fe is ready to take her as soon as we can arrange to get her there."

"Hold on, Harper," a deep voice from the back of the room called out. Everyone turned their heads to see Mayor Adams making his way up the aisle. "What's all this about?"

"Mayor!" Harper backed up a step and ran his finger around his collar. "We weren't expecting you back until next week."

"I finished my business back East earlier than expected," the mayor said, continuing up the aisle. "It would appear I returned in the nick of time. What's this about you trying to make Emma Hanson give up the child she promised to raise?"

Harper's smirk disappeared as the mayor joined him on the podium. A fine bead of perspiration formed on his upper lip. He pulled a handkerchief from his jacket pocket and mopped his face. "I—we—the council thought a single woman, particularly one trying to run a business—"

"From what I've heard since I got back into town," the mayor said with a nod at Emma, "Mandy Drake is in very capable hands."

Harper glared at Emma and cleared his throat. "I just thought that a married couple would be better able to—"

"That's not quite true." Sheriff Haynes traipsed up the aisle. "What you thought, Mr. Harper, was that you could run Miss Hanson out of town so you could buy her place of business."

The crowd began to murmur.

"I–I did no such thing!" Harper shrieked over the din.

"So that's what this was all about," Homer Williams said, rising from the table. He squinted at the mayor. "He's been going on and on about how valuable all the property close to the train station will be, once the line gets finished on into Amarillo in the next year or so. He must've had this plan in mind the whole time."

"That's preposterous!" Harper bellowed.

Jed Brewster stood and addressed the crowd. "No, it isn't." He glanced down at his wife, Laura, and she clasped his hand

He turned toward Emma. "Douglas Harper wanted to scare you out of town, Miss Emma. He paid me to come in drunk that night and cause a disturbance. Then he tried to pay me to throw a rock through your window. I turned him down."

Harper's face turned bright red. "No one is going to believe you, you drunk."

"Well, maybe they'll believe me," Zeke Anderson said. "I went in to the sheriff's office this afternoon and confessed to throwing that rock into the café and setting that fire, too. And I told them about you paying me to do them things." He turned toward Emma. "I'm real sorry, Miss Hanson. I promise I'll make full restitution for all the damage I done."

Harper turned suddenly and ran out the side door. He returned a moment later, backing up, Deputy Carmichael's gun held to his chest. Sheriff Haynes quickly slapped handcuffs on the banker and led him down the aisle through the tittering crowd.

"Sheriff, wait," Emma said.

The sheriff stopped and pulled Harper around to face her.

"Councilman Harper, there's something I'd like to know. What made you think you'd get my place if I left town?"

Harper shrugged. "It would have been easy to find someone to buy your property for me."

Robert Morris, the real estate dabbler, called out from the back of the room. "He paid me to make Miss Emma an offer on her place of business if she decided to sell. He didn't tell me he was trying to scare her into doing it."

"Well, Mr. Harper here isn't going to be doing much wheelin' and dealin' anymore." Sheriff Haynes led him out the door, amid cheers from the crowd.

The noise grew so loud, the mayor had to bang the gavel.

"Before we call an end to this meeting," he said when the noise finally died down, "I'd like to apologize to Miss Hanson on behalf of the town council. . ." He gave the men at the table a wilting look. ". . .for causing her so much misery these past few weeks."

"Thank you, sir," Emma said. "But all I'd really like is an end to all this. Since the council started this trouble, I'd like for them to formally proclaim that I have the legal right to keep Mandy Drake and raise her as my own child."

The other councilmen huddled together for a mere minute before Homer Williams stood. "Miss Emma, we're all agreed that's the least we can do for you. You have full and complete custody of Mandy Drake—and you don't have to have a husband to keep her."

"Too late for that, Councilman," Matt called out, making his way up the aisle to Emma's side. He put an arm around her waist and pulled her close. "She's already found one. Minister Turley married us this afternoon, and we invite you all back to the café right now to join in our celebration. Ben and Hallie have been busy all day, and they've prepared quite a spread."

Amid cheers and clapping, Matt kissed his bride. Emma returned the kiss, thanking the Lord above for making sure she kept a promise made.

A Letter To Our Readers

Dear Reader:

In order that we might better contribute to your reading enjoyment, we would appreciate your taking a few minutes to respond to the following questions. We welcome your comments and read each form and letter we receive. When completed, please return to the following:

Fiction Editor
Heartsong Presents
PO Box 719
Uhrichsville, Ohio 44683

Did you enjoy reading *A Promise Made* by Janet Lee Barton?
❏ Very much! I would like to see more books by this author!
❏ Moderately. I would have enjoyed it more if

_____

_____

_____

Are you a member of **Heartsong Presents**?   ❏ Yes   ❏ No
If no, where did you purchase this book? _____

_____

How would you rate, on a scale from 1 (poor) to 5 (superior), the cover design? _____

On a scale from 1 (poor) to 10 (superior), please rate the following elements.

____ Heroine	____ Plot
____ Hero	____ Inspirational theme
____ Setting	____ Secondary characters

5. These characters were special because?_____

_____

_____

6. How has this book inspired your life?_____

_____

_____

7. What settings would you like to see covered in future
   Heartsong Presents books? _____

_____

_____

8. What are some inspirational themes you would like to see
   treated in future books? _____

_____

_____

9. Would you be interested in reading other **Heartsong
   Presents** titles? ❑ Yes ❑ No

10. Please check your age range:
   ❑ Under 18   ❑ 18-24
   ❑ 25-34   ❑ 35-45
   ❑ 46-55   ❑ Over 55

Name_____

Occupation _____

Address _____

City_____ State_____ Zip_____

Minnesota

*I*n 1877, the citizens of Chippewa Falls, Minnesota, are recovering from the devastation of a five-year grasshopper infestation. Throughout the years that follow, countless hardships, trials, and life-threatening dangers will plague the settlers as they struggle for survival amidst the harsh environs and crude conditions f the state's southwest plains.

Historical, paperback, 480 pages, 5³/₁₆" x 8"

❤ ❤ ❤ ❤ ❤ ❤ ❤ ❤ ❤ ❤ ❤ ❤ ❤ ❤ ❤

❤ ❤ ❤ ❤ ❤ ❤ ❤ ❤ ❤ ❤ ❤ ❤ ❤ ❤ ❤

Presents

Great Inspirational Romance at a Great Price!

Heartsong Presents books are inspirational romances in contemporary and historical settings, designed to give you an enjoyable, spirit-lifting reading experience. You can choose wonderfully written titles from some of today's best authors like Peggy Darty, Sally Laity, Tracie Peterson, Colleen L. Reece, Debra White Smith, and many others.

When ordering quantities less than twelve, above titles are $3.25 each.
Not all titles may be available at time of order.

ℋEARTSONG ❤ PRESENTS

Love Stories
Are Rated G!

That's for godly, gratifying, and of course, great! If you love a thrilling love story but don't appreciate the sordidness of some popular paperback romances, **Heartsong Presents** is for you. In fact, **Heartsong Presents** is the only inspirational romance book club featuring love stories where Christian faith is the primary ingredient in a marriage relationship.

Sign up today to receive your first set of four, never-before published Christian romances. Send no money now; you will receive a bill with the first shipment. You may cancel at any time without obligation, and if you aren't completely satisfied with any selection, you may return the books for an immediate refund!

Imagine. . .four new romances every four weeks—two historical, two contemporary—with men and women like you who long to meet the one God has chosen as the love of their lives. . .all for the low price of $10.99 postpaid.

To join, simply complete the coupon below and mail to the address provided. **Heartsong Presents** romances are rated G for another reason: They'll arrive Godspeed!

YES! Sign me up for Heart❤ng!

NEW MEMBERSHIPS WILL BE SHIPPED IMMEDIATELY!
Send no money now. We'll bill you only $10.99 postpaid with your first shipment of four books. Or for faster action, call toll free 1-800-847-8270.

NAME _____

ADDRESS _____

CITY _____ STATE _____ ZIP _____

MAIL TO: HEARTSONG PRESENTS, P.O. Box 721, Uhrichsville, Ohio 4468
or visit www.heartsongpresents.com